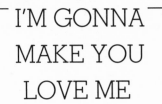

I'M GONNA
MAKE YOU
LOVE ME

THE STORY OF
DIANA ROSS

I'M GONNA MAKE YOU LOVE ME

by JAMES HASKINS

The Dial Press NEW YORK

Published by The Dial Press
1 Dag Hammarskjold Plaza / New York, New York 10017

ACKNOWLEDGMENTS

I am grateful to Laurel Burns and J. M. Stifle and to Jean
Currie, Curator of the E. Azalia Hackley Collection of the
Detroit Public Library for their help in gathering material for
this book. A special thank-you to Kathy Benson for her help.

Excerpts from "Why Diana Ross Left the Supremes" by
Louie Robinson reprinted by permission of *Ebony* magazine,
copyright 1970 by Johnson Publishing Company, Inc.

Excerpts from "The Girls from Motown" reprinted by permission
from *Time*, The Weekly Newsmagazine, copyright Time, Inc., 1966.

Excerpts from "Off the Record with the Supremes" by Edwin Miller
reprinted from *Seventeen*® magazine, copyright © 1966 by
Triangle Communications, Inc. All rights reserved.

Excerpts from "The Lady Isn't Singing" and "Diana Reigns
Supreme" by Robert Wahls, copyright 1973 and 1976 respectively,
New York News, Inc., reprinted by permission.

Excerpts from *Diana Ross, Supreme Lady*, copyright 1978 by
Connie Berman, reprinted by permission.

"I'm Gonna Make You Love Me," music by Ken Gamble, words by
Jerry Ross, words and music by Jerry Williams, copyright
© 1966, 1978 by Act Three Music and Downstairs Music,
Unichappell Music, Inc., Administrator.

Photographs appear courtesy of:

frontispiece: Johnson Publishing Company (Leroy Patton)
pp. 91, 92, 93: Johnson Publishing Company (G. Marshall Wilson)
p. 94: Wide World Photos / pp. 95, 96: Douglas Kirkland / Contact

Library of Congress Cataloging in Publication Data

Haskins, James, 1941– / I'm gonna make you love me.

Discography: p.
Summary / Traces the life of singer Diana Ross from
her early years in a Detroit ghetto to Hollywood.
1. Ross, Diana, 1944–   —Juvenile literature.
2. Singers—United States—Biography—Juvenile literature.
[1. Ross, Diana, 1944–   2. Singers.
3. Afro-Americans—Biography]   I. Title.
ML3903.R67H4   784'.092'4   [B]   [92]   79–3586
ISBN 0-8037-4213-4

CONTENTS

GROWING UP
IN THE
BLACK BOTTOM

It is November 8, 1979, and the huge Radio City Music Hall in New York City is packed to overflowing with people who have spent a lot of money to get in. Even tickets for the Third Mezzanine are $10.50, and from back there you can see about as well as you can from the North Pole. But this is a very special night, and people are willing to sit anywhere just to say they saw Diana Ross in her exclusive one-night engagement at Radio City.

To see Diana Ross in person is really to see *somebody*. Her latest album, *The Boss*, has made the Top Twenty, and the critics like it as much as record-buyers do. But a lot of people in the audience don't really care if she sings or not. They just want to see her and to feel the magic that somehow surrounds her whenever and wherever she appears. No one has ever been able to completely explain that kind of magic except to say that if you have it, you're a superstar. And Diana Ross is a superstar.

She proves it this evening at Radio City. She is glamorous

and can wear outrageous costumes the way few others can; she sings and dances and cracks jokes. She makes the audience believe that she is having a wonderful time and invites them to share it with her. And when they leave, every member of the audience—from those in the $22.50 seats to those in the $10.50 seats way up in the Third Mezzanine—are saying to themselves and to one another, "Now, *that's* entertainment."

Diana Ross seems so sure of herself, so naturally glamorous, that it's hard to believe that she was once, as she puts it, just "a skinny kid from the Detroit projects," a kid who was not glamorous and not sure of herself at all. She was poor and shy and felt like a nobody. In fact the only thing she had going for her was a fierce determination to be *somebody*. How she got to be somebody when just about everything seemed to be against her is quite a story.

The name Detroit automatically means cars to most Americans, and to many non-Americans too. For nearly a century, ever since Henry Ford set up his business there, this city on the southeast edge of Michigan across the Detroit River from Windsor, Ontario, Canada, has been the center of American automobile production. But before that, because of its location between Lake Erie and Lake St. Clair, connected to both by the Detroit River, Detroit was already a major industrial center. Iron and steel, boots and shoes, chemicals and railroad cars were all important products made in Detroit before 1896, when the first "horseless carriage" was driven through the city streets by

2

a local businessman named Charles B. King. So when the United States entered World War II in 1941, Detroit was one of the major sources America looked to for materials and products for the war effort. In turn the industries of Detroit looked to the rest of America to supply the manpower for its factories. They got a lot of that manpower from the South.

Southern Blacks were drawn to Detroit like steel filings to a magnet. Not only were there plenty of jobs, but living conditions were better too. There was discrimination in the North, but it was not as brutal as the segregation below the Mason-Dixon line. In the South most Blacks had no hope of getting ahead in life. Northern cities like Detroit seemed to offer them a better chance. And so Fred and Ernestine Ross moved to Detroit from Alabama in the early 1940s; Fred got a job on the assembly line of the American Brass Company, and they started their family.

Diana, born March 26, 1944, was the second child in a family of six. She was christened Diane Ross, but somehow the name went down as Diana on her birth certificate. Her mother was not pleased about that mistake, but she never went to the trouble of getting the certificate changed. She saw no need to do so. Everyone called the baby Diane, and Diana Ross is still Diane to her family and best friends.

At the time Diana was born, the Rosses lived in a third-floor walk-up in what Diana calls a "raggedy old apartment house" in a Black section that today would be called a ghetto. Then it was called "the Black Bottom" or simply "the neighborhood." The Rosses could not afford a better place to live. Fred Ross was working steadily at American Brass, but prices were higher in Detroit than in Alabama, and as the years passed, there were more and more mouths to feed.

In no time at all, or so it seemed, Diana and her older sister, Barbara, had three brothers and another sister. Since the apartment was small, all the children slept together in one bedroom, the girls in one bed and the boys in the other. In the summertime there was always a jar of kerosene lighted to keep the chinch bugs away, and a lot of tossing and turning and squabbling about who was to sleep closest to the window and enjoy the occasional breeze that cut through the heat and humidity. During the winter the Ross children huddled together in their beds, grateful for the extra warmth, for the house was not very well insulated, and the wind howled through the cracks around the windows. They spent their winter days in the kitchen, for Mrs. Ross was almost always cooking something, and the heat from the oven made the kitchen the warmest room in the house.

It wasn't the best family to get individual attention in. To make ends meet Fred Ross had to take on extra jobs, so even when he wasn't working at American Brass, he was out working as a mechanic somewhere. Ernestine Ross was always so busy tending to the youngest children and cooking and cleaning that she didn't have much time to listen or talk to the older children. Little Diana felt that lack of attention, and like a lot of other middle children, she resented it.

4

She wasn't the oldest. The oldest, Barbara, was a quiet girl who was very good about helping and who never gave her parents any trouble. Diana sensed that her parents often wished she were more like Barbara. Nor was she the youngest. In fact she'd graduated from being the baby of the family to being an older sister when she was hardly more than a baby herself. She was expected to help with the little ones and act more grown-up than they did, but that usually didn't make her feel more grown-up. Most of the time it just made her feel put-upon. It seemed to her that if you weren't the oldest or the youngest, you weren't much of anything.

She was very young when she first started going out on her own. "I would walk a long, long way out of the neighborhood, away from Mama, just to see what the rest of the world looked like," Diana recalls. If she was like most other children, and she probably was, sometimes when she took these long walks she was trying out the idea of running away. She always came back though, and Mrs. Ross, in spite of having her hands full with all her children, probably knew what her second daughter was doing. But she never scolded Diana. Instead she let her try out independence.

The Rosses encouraged their children to be independent. They would have to be. It wasn't an easy life for Black people, even up North in Detroit in the 1940s. Fred Ross saw white workers get promotions even though he was a better worker than many of them. He saw them get the first offers for overtime work that would bring in extra money his family badly needed. He and his wife didn't have many dreams for the future except to be able to afford a better place to live and not to have to worry so much about money all the time, but even those dreams were hard to realize. They hoped—but didn't take for granted—that things would be better for their children, and they knew that if their children were to have a better chance in life, they would first have to learn to take care of themselves and second, have to learn to be the best at whatever they tried to do.

Although she didn't completely understand the reasons why, it didn't take Diana long to figure out that the best way to get attention was to be good at something. So she became good at singing. There was always music in the house. One of Diana's happiest early memories is of the times when her mother would take a break from housework, put on some Billie Holiday records, and sit down on her red-velvet couch—her most prized possession—to listen. Those were the times when Diana could climb up on the couch and sit with her mother and enjoy some practically undivided attention for a few moments before some sister or brother woke up from a nap or came in crying. At other times Mrs. Ross would listen to the radio and sing along with the popular tunes while she worked. Diana would listen, too, and by the time she was five or six she could sing along with the radio tunes. Both her mother and father were delighted that she had such a good voice and would ask Diana to sing when company came. Diana loved being the center of attention and wished company would come more often.

About that time, when she was six, Diana decided that she would like a pair of black patent-leather shoes, but Mr. Ross just didn't have the money to buy them. This bothered him a lot, and it wasn't very far in the back of his mind when some relatives came to visit. As usual, Diana wanted to sing. This particular time she sang "In the Still of the Night" and as her father saw how much the relatives enjoyed her performance he got an idea. He passed the hat and collected enough money to buy her patent-leather shoes, which probably gave Diana the idea that singing brought not only attention but more tangible good things as well.

Diana also excelled in athletics. She was lucky enough to attend the only elementary school in Detroit that had a swimming pool, and she took advantage of that by learning to swim so well that she won all the swimming contests she entered. Her teachers couldn't believe she could be so skinny and yet so strong. In fact, she was so skinny that they always made her take a nap after the free lunch, since you're supposed to gain weight by sleeping after a meal. At the annual American Brass employee picnics she always won the footraces, even beating the boys, and around the neighborhood she could climb fences and rob apple trees with the best of them. While her older sister, Barbara, grew into a quiet young girl who liked to read books, Diana became a tomboy—and proud of it. She was absolutely fearless when it came to defending her younger brothers and sisters from the bullies in the neighborhood. She had plenty of fights with her sisters and brothers, because as they got older it didn't get any easier living in such close quarters and sleeping in the same room. But they always stuck together during fights with other children. They were a very close-knit family.

When Diana was about nine, the family had to split up for a while. Ernestine Ross became seriously ill with tuberculosis and had to go to a sanitarium in Holland, Michigan. Their father was at work all day and could not care for the children properly. So the children were sent to Alabama to stay with their grandparents. Diana's grandfather, the Reverend William Moton, was pastor of the Alabama Bessemer Baptist Church and one of the leaders of the Black community in Bessemer.

In the South at that time Blacks were almost completely segregated from whites. By law they had to ride in the backs of buses, go to separate schools, drink from separate drinking fountains, and use separate rest rooms. There were white restaurants and Black restaurants, and those restaurants that served both races had to have separate entrances and high partitions between the white and Black dining areas. One southern state even had a law that said Black people and white people couldn't play checkers together. In 1954, during the year Diana and the other Ross children lived in Alabama, the United States Supreme Court handed down a very important ruling, which declared "separate but equal" schools unconstitutional. The schools in question were the segregated schools in the South, not the ones like Diana's school in Detroit. Her elementary school was almost all Black, but that was a different kind of segregation. Called "de facto" segregation, it was segregation in fact rather than by law. The school was almost all Black because it was in a mostly Black neighborhood. If the Rosses had been able to afford to live in a white neighborhood—and if they had been allowed to live in that white neighborhood—school officials in Detroit would have had no choice but to allow the Ross children to go to a mostly white school in the neighborhood. In the South a Black family could live right next door to a school, but if it was a white school the children in that family could not go to it. Instead they had to go to a Black school, no matter how far away it was. And they would have to get there any way they could, since only white children could ride on the school buses. (The idea of busing schoolchildren far away from their homes is not new; southern white children used to be bused to white schools miles away all the time.) The white schools and Black schools were supposed to be equal in quality—"separate but equal"—but that was not so. The Black schools always got cast-off textbooks from the white schools; the Black children who lived miles away from their school had to walk, while white children could ride buses. That is why the Supreme Court declared the separate schools unconstitutional.

The other "separate" things, like restaurants and rest rooms and drinking fountains, were not "equal" either, and in later years the civil rights movement and civil rights laws passed by the federal government integrated these too. But when Diana Ross was in Alabama, everything was still segregated, and no matter how respected her family was, they still had to stay in their "place."

Diana had heard how things were in the South. Her parents sometimes spoke about it, and most of her friends had relatives in the South and had visited them there. But that still did not prepare her for her first experience of segregation. No one can really be prepared for that. Diana remembers having to drink from water fountains marked COLORED, having to go into public places through back doors, and not being able to go to certain places, like restaurants, at all. She did not understand why she had to wait until she found a "colored" rest room when a "white" rest room was right nearby. She did not understand why her grandmother had to go to the back of a store and wait to be helped while white customers who came in after her could enter by the front door and be helped right away. She didn't understand why she had to step aside and let white people pass on the sidewalk. But every time she asked about all this, she didn't get very clear answers. It was the way things were, she was told, but she wasn't told why things had to be that way. It troubled her not to know. It troubled her even more to have a secret suspicion that there was something wrong with her because she was Black, and to be unable to talk to anyone about it. She wished she could show those white people that she was just as good as they were.

On top of all this, it was hard being away from her home and her parents. Fred Ross tried to make up for the separation by sending great presents that Christmas—all the girls got majorette boots—but the present the Ross children

10

wanted most did not arrive until some months later when word came from Detroit that at last their mother was well and the family could be together again. Diana had no regrets about leaving Alabama and getting back home, where you didn't have to worry about being downtown and having to go to the bathroom and where you could sit anywhere on the bus you wanted to.

Back home Diana felt the need to talk with her parents about segregation in the South, but as usual they were too busy to spend much time with her. She tried talking with her friends, but those who had never been to the South didn't really understand what she was talking about, and those who had been, didn't like remembering. "You're back up North now," they told her. "Don't worry about it." And pretty soon Bessemer, Alabama, seemed very far away to her too. Besides, she had to get busy catching up on the "latest things" that were going on in Detroit. The kids were using expressions she had never heard in Alabama. More importantly they were singing and dancing to a kind of music called rock 'n' roll that she had not heard in Alabama, although, her Detroit friends assured her, it had been playing on the radio for ages. "That's the trouble with the South," her friends would say, echoing their parents. Actually, the songs her Detroit friends were singing and humming and listening to on the radio were pretty new to them too. Real rock and roll—or rock 'n' roll, as it was usually called—had just become popular in 1953, when Diana was nine and down South.

The makings of rock 'n' roll had been around for a long

11

time in Black jazz and blues. But it was in the early 1950s that young white performers began to incorporate those basically Black rhythms and to attract a wide audience. "Crazy, Man, Crazy" by Bill Haley and the Comets, the first rock 'n' roll song to make the best-selling lists on *Billboard* magazine's national charts, was released in 1953. That record was quickly followed by others, like "Money, Honey" by the Drifters and "Good Lovin'" by the Clovers. These records were also released in 1953, a year in which six records that can be classified as rock 'n' roll became popular. By 1954 the rock 'n' roll sound had really caught on, and fourteen records with that sound made the charts; in 1955 "Rock Around the Clock" by Bill Haley and the Comets became the first rock 'n' roll song ever to reach the No. 1 spot on the national charts. But rock 'n' roll first became popular in the cities of the North, and so naturally that is where it could most often be heard on local radio stations. It took another couple of years for the music to reach the southern rural areas.

Diana didn't want to seem out of touch and spent hours listening to the radio so she could sing and hum the latest hits and know the names of all the big rock 'n' roll groups. Most of the hit songs in those days were recorded by groups like Frankie Lymon and the Teenagers, the Dells, and Little Anthony and the Imperials.

Music was important to Diana and her friends. That was partly because it was important to everyone around them. Their parents and older brothers and sisters listened to it and danced to it and sang to it, and so they did too. But mainly, for kids like Diana, it was important because they really loved to sing and dance and move to its rhythms. Diana can't remember a time when she didn't love music. First there were her mother's Billie Holiday records, and Diana associated the rhythm and the sound of the singer's voice with warmth and love and attention. And then there were all those popular songs her mother listened to on the radio—the kind we now call easy-listening music. And finally there was church music. On Sundays, when they went to the Olivet Baptist Church, the entire Ross family, or at least all who were old enough, sang in the choir, carrying on an old tradition in Mrs. Ross's family. Her parents, the Reverend and Mrs. Moton, and all twelve of their children had been brought up in the church and singing in the choir. So Diana came naturally by her love for singing. And except for the instruction she received from the church choir director, from school music teachers, and from her friends, Diana learned what she knew all by herself.

Not long after the children returned from the South, the Ross family moved from one home to another in Detroit's "Black Bottom," exchanging the apartment in a house with a backyard for a newer apartment in a high-rise, low-income project. The move was not hard on Diana, because she already knew many of the children who lived in the projects. Some, like Florence Ballard and Mary Wilson, went to the same elementary school as Diana did. Others she knew from church. So she didn't have to worry about being a new kid. She also didn't have to worry about being poorer than the other kids (something she'd started to become aware of since entering school), because the Brewster-Douglass Projects was a place where, according to Diana, "you have to be poor just to get in."

The Ross family received no direct government aid like welfare or food stamps, and with six growing children both Mr. and Mrs. Ross had to work hard to make ends meet. By the 1950s a Black man who was a good worker could be promoted and Fred Ross had been made foreman at American Brass. He was also an important member of the union to which the company's workers belonged and he still did odd jobs as a mechanic. As soon as her older children started school and she found someone to take care of Chico, the youngest, Ernestine Ross went to work as a maid for an "up-tee-doo" white family, as Diana puts it. Still, Mr. Ross insisted that his children have a great Christmas each year. One year they all got bikes; another year it was a television. But there were not many luxuries the rest of the year. Mrs. Ross recalls, "We were eating, and that's pretty good. In the project you got along according to how many children you had. There was twelve in Florence's family, there was three in Mary's, and there was six in ours. So Mary was the best off, Florence the worst, and we were in the middle."

By the time the Rosses moved to the projects, Diana was beginning to realize what she had and what she didn't have, and getting a television didn't help. All those commercials showing things her parents couldn't afford, all those beautiful clothes the women wore, all those comfortable homes the people lived in made Diana wish her family had more money. Then, too, the television people who had all these things were almost exclusively white. Except for Eddie "Rochester" Anderson on *The Jack Benny Show*, there was hardly a Black face to be seen on television in those days, and that fact did not escape the attention of Black people. To the grown-ups it was just another example of white discrimination, but to a young Black girl it seemed to underscore the idea that somehow there was something wrong with her and that because she was Black, she was a nobody.

DIANA JOINS
THE PRIMETTES

$\mathbf{D}$iana's life changed after she graduated from junior high school. Detroit youngsters went to high school not according to where they lived but based on their grades and skills. Diana had made good grades in junior high; she had also shown skill at drawing. So while most of her friends went to Northwestern High, she went to Cass Technical High School, where students had to have a B+ average to get in and where they could take drawing and design courses.

Diana was very interested in design. From the time she was very young, she was aware of colors and the textures of fabrics—like the red-velvet couch in the family living room. As she got older and started thinking about a career, she decided that she liked fashion design. She also decided she would like to become a model.

But her first two years at Cass Tech were not happy ones. Kids from all over the city went to that school, and in fact it was predominantly white. It was the first time Diana had come into close contact with whites, and she was very unsure of herself around them. Her experiences with segregation in the South when she was nine had left a deep impression. She was distrustful of the white students. She was also embarrassed about living in the projects and not having as much money or as many clothes as the other students seemed to have. She remembers, "I thought everybody thought they were better than me." It was very hard for her to leave a junior high school where she knew almost everybody and where she was popular to go to a new school where she felt like an outsider.

Feeling the way she did, she wasn't likely to enjoy the schoolwork very much. As a freshman and sophomore, she had to take more English and history and math than art or design courses, and she was not very interested in these subjects. "I didn't like to sit down and study, and nobody ever taught me a system. I'd watch TV while I studied. I never had anyplace to go. I'd try the public library, but it was like boredom."

Diana had never read books as a child, and her mother had never had time to read to her. "The excitement of making pictures by reading—I didn't get that," Diana explains. At a time when she really needed it, Diana had no escape. She was unhappy at school. At home she felt as if her family was closing in on her. Her parents were not getting along very well, and she sometimes felt uncomfortable being around them. She was frightened when they argued. Some of her friends' parents were divorced, and she was afraid that might happen to her own parents. She started spending a lot of time in the streets.

There were gangs out in the streets. The most powerful local gang was the Shakers, whose girl friends were called the Shakerettes. But Diana was never attracted to their violent brand of "kicks," even though she sometimes envied the gang members because they seemed so sure of themselves. There were pimps and prostitutes in the neighborhood, and like other kids Diana envied the money and the clothes and the glamor they seemed to have. "We kind of knew what they were doing, but not really," she says. "They were nice people. It was a profession, you know. It would've been easy for me. Because it's difficult to figure out ways to get out of what the white man calls 'the ghetto.' . . . I knew a lot of pimps. It's a possibility if I had got strung out over one of those guys, it could've been me. If I had fallen in love. . . ."

In those days, if they wanted to stay on the right side of the law, Black kids thought they could get out of the ghetto in two basic ways—through sports or through music. In the 1950s Black youngsters did not have many idols to look up to who were not in one or the other of those fields. Nowadays the mayor of Detroit is Black, and so are the mayors of many other cities. There has been a Black U.S. ambassador to the United Nations and there are Blacks in Congress. There are Black television and movie stars, and Black models by the score. But back in the 1950s, when Black kids tried to think about Black people who had made it, just about the only people they could think of were athletes or entertainers.

A lot of the older boys in the neighborhood hoped to

become boxers, because boxing had been open to Blacks for decades, and several Black boxers like Jack Johnson and Joe Louis had become very famous. Almost everyone played baseball—well, not exactly baseball, because no one could afford the equipment, but stickball—because Jackie Robinson had integrated the major leagues three years after Diana was born. And more and more boys were playing basketball because Blacks could now play in the professional basketball league too. Everyone knew about the Harlem Globetrotters, of course, because they'd been around for a long time, but they were an all-Black team that played exhibition basketball. During the 1950–51 season both the Boston Celtics and the New York Knickerbockers had taken on Black players, and by the late 1950s there were a number of Black players on the pro teams. For every one who made it there were thousands of young Blacks who began to hope they could make it too. The basketball courts in the Detroit projects were busy all the time.

Both girls and boys did a lot of singing, because the entertainment field had been open to Blacks for a long time, too, and by the 1950s several Black singing groups had become popular. Just about anywhere you went in the projects, especially during warm weather, you could find a group of teen-agers singing in harmony the latest popular songs. Many of the groups were very good, and a local promoter decided to take advantage of all the untapped musical talent in the Black neighborhoods of Detroit.

He found a group of boys who sang well together and

19

started booking them at local record hops. The group, called the Primes, was so popular that the promoter started looking around for a female group. One of the Primes was a young man named Eddie Kendricks. He told the man about a group of girls in the Brewster projects who also sang well together, and it was not long before the man had signed the girls up and the Primettes were born.

The first group of Primettes did not include Diana Ross, although it did include one of her best friends. Mary Wilson and Diana liked to sew together. Diana's mother would bring home dresses her employer had given her, and Diana and Mary would make them over so they could wear them. Another of the first Primettes was Florence Ballard, a quiet girl who was close friends with Mary and who wanted to be a nurse. The idea of forming a singing group had been hers, and she had asked Mary and two other girls to join her. One was named Barbara Martin. The other one lasted such a short time that her name is never mentioned. Her leaving made it possible for Diana to join the group.

When Diana found out that Mary was in a singing group that had actually been signed up by a promoter, she really envied her friend. To be in a group was the biggest thing that could happen to you; practically all the other kids would have given their eye teeth for a chance to sing at a local record hop or maybe on the radio. It made Mary somebody, and Diana was downright jealous. But she realized it wasn't Mary's fault that Florence had asked her and not Diana to be in the group. Mary probably knew how Diana felt, and so when the other girl dropped out,

20

she talked the other Primettes into giving her friend a try.

Diana said yes before Mary got the words out of her mouth. Mary explained that Diana was not automatically in. They'd have to see if her voice would work with those of the other girls. Mary was lead singer, and her backup singers had to be able to harmonize well together. If Diana's voice fit in, she would be accepted. Diana decided that she would fit in. With Mary's help she practiced the songs the group usually sang. Then she practiced with the group. They all agreed they sounded good together, but the original Primettes weren't going to take any chances on blowing their big opportunity. They decided to give a public performance. So one evening Mary, Florence, Barbara, and Diana went out into the streets of the Brewster-Douglass Projects and began to sing, immediately drawing a small and very knowledgeable crowd. The Brewster projects people knew their music, and if the girls had sounded bad, their audience would have let them know immediately. Instead the audience began to snap their fingers and tap their feet. Someone passed the hat, and the girls were presented with three whole dollars. Diana Ross was in.

She was so excited that she could not wait to tell her family. Her brothers and sisters were as excited as she was. Her mother was pleased. Her father wanted to know where she would be singing. "Oh, at parties and things," Diana answered. What kind of parties? her parents wanted to know, and Diana could not tell them. She had not thought past getting into the group.

It turned out that the Primettes were expected to sing at parties and hops all over town, and Diana's father did not like to have her going out of the neighborhood at night. So she lied. She would say she was going over to Mary's or to the home of some other girl friend. Arriving home late at night, she would find her father waiting for her, and she would be punished. But Diana was determined to continue to be a Primette. Like the other girls, she didn't care if she got paid or not; all she cared about was performing. She had found a way to be "somebody," and after a time her father understood that she was not sneaking out at night to do anything but sing. He decided to trust her and to let her go her own way, just as he and his wife had done when Diana was a small child.

Florence also ran into problems at home when she started spending a lot of time singing at parties with the Primettes. Her father, who had been a worker for Chevrolet, had died when she was young and as head of the family; her older brother felt it was his responsibility to see that she got her education. When her grades went down one semester, he decided it was because of her singing with the Primettes. He ordered her to quit the group and pay more attention to her homework.

Florence was heartsick, and so were Diana and Mary and Barbara. The other girls could have found a replacement for Florence, but they were loyal friends. After all, it was Florence who had first come up with the idea of starting a group and who had persuaded Mary and the others to join her. But Diana was terribly afraid the group would break up altogether, and she just couldn't let that happen. It meant too much to her. She even called Florence's brother to try to get him to change his mind; that took a lot of courage since they were all afraid of him. But his decision was firm. For the next few weeks all four girls walked around gloomily, resenting this horrible twist of fate. Eventually, Florence's brother gave in, and the Primettes joyfully regrouped and were on their way.

That was not the end of the problems Florence caused the group. There were times when she simply did not show up for singing dates or for rehearsals and she seemed to have no good excuse. She did have a lot of family problems as the middle child among five brothers and six sisters. Without a father they had a hard time keeping peace in the family and making ends meet. But if the group had really been important to her, Florence would have found a way to make those dates and rehearsals. She did not have the same drive as the others did; in fact, although it was she who had started the group, she was the least committed to making it a success. Still the others never seriously talked about replacing her, although they became very exasperated with her at times.

Singing with the Primettes made a great difference in Diana's life. The group made very little money—often they did not get paid at all—but what they got in attention made up for it. Their names were actually mentioned on a local radio station from time to time! For Diana being a Primette meant feeling secure, feeling confident. "I was doing something at last when I started singing," she says.

23

"The kids noticed me. I cut my hair in a bob and I gained weight and wore nylons and high heels. Then I found out that if you think you're somebody, you *are* somebody. When I walked down the hall, I'd say, 'Hi, Bob,' 'Hi, Timmy.' I must have said hi a thousand times, I had so many friends."

She even had the courage to cut up a bit in school, something she would never have thought of doing before. Rita Griffin, who now writes for the *Michigan Chronicle*, was in a sewing class with Diana back at Cass Tech, and she remembers that every time the clothing instructor left the room, Diana and two other girls named Delphine and Gwen would start harmonizing. They would entertain the rest of the class until the instructor reentered the room and cast a stern look toward the back of the class where the three girls sat.

Diana still loved designing and sewing clothes, and she had taken over the job of designing the Primettes' costumes. Of course the girls did not have a lot of money to spend on clothes, but Diana felt it was important for their clothing to match in some way when they sang together, and so she would get the others to shop the sales with her so they could buy matching blouses or dresses in the same pattern but in different colors. She would watch for fabric bargains so she could buy material for matching skirts, which she and Mary would run up on the school's sewing machine after school. Diana's sewing and designing talents found their greatest expression in this activity now. She also went to charm school at Hudson's department store downtown on Saturdays, with an eye toward modeling, and went to cosmetology school at night during her junior year. But since she had started singing with the Primettes, her ideas about her future had started to change. She had discovered that she enjoyed singing even more than sewing and designing and modeling, and she especially loved performing. The once shy teen-ager loved being in front of an audience as much as she had as a child, loved to see them begin to snap their fingers and tap their feet to the music she made, loved to hear their applause.

She did not get much support at home. Her father still did not approve of her singing at parties and hops outside the neighborhood at night. Her mother encouraged her love for singing but was quite certain that her ideas about a career in music were just part of a stage, and that eventually she would settle down to a more solid career. Nor did many of the teachers at Cass Tech encourage her. It was still a time when career possibilities for young Black people were limited, and probably many of the teachers had the same attitude toward Diana's hopes that her parents did: Even with all kinds of talent she had very little chance to succeed, and so she should concentrate on preparing for a career that she could reasonably expect to have. There was even one teacher who, at least in Diana's opinion, did not even think she had much talent. He was the teacher who directed the Cass Tech musical.

Loving to perform the way she did, Diana wanted very much to be in one of the plays Cass Tech presented, and when she learned that the new play was to be a musical, she was even more eager to be a part of it. So she tried out. "I sang 'Ebb Tide,' " she recalls, "and after I finished, the teacher said I had a pretty good voice, but not for this kind of thing, maybe something else. In other words, he wanted to tell me, 'You're not really good, forget it.' "

In all fairness to this teacher, who probably has since come in for a lot of ribbing as "the teacher who said Diana Ross wasn't good enough," it should be pointed out that he was directing a stage musical and that it takes a very strong voice to come across onstage. The actors in a musical do not use microphones, and so they have to have powerful voices to make themselves heard throughout the hall. Diana's voice was not that powerful, and even if it had been, that power would not have come across in a slow ballad like "Ebb Tide." Had she chosen a rip-roaring, upbeat song, she might have been more successful at the tryouts. But Diana did not stop to think about what she might have done wrong. She expected to be a success at whatever she tried. So she decided that the teacher-director didn't know what he was talking about and grew more determined than ever to be a success.

By the time they were juniors, the Primettes were looking toward bigger things than singing at local record hops, where they never made much money. They wanted to get into the big time and make records and have money to buy fancy costumes and help their families. So they decided to audition for a new local record company called Hitsville, USA. The Primes had recently auditioned for Hitsville and were pretty sure they would get a contract. In the spring of 1960 the Primettes dressed in matching costumes and went to the recording studio at 2457 Woodward Avenue. They were so frightened that their teeth chattered, but the Primettes were determined to make a good impression. They had launched into "There Goes My Baby" by the Drifters when Berry Gordy, Jr., head of Hitsville, walked in.

Diana remembers, "When Berry walked in, he wasn't looking like the Berry we expected. He looked like a kid." For his part Berry Gordy didn't just think the girls auditioning looked like kids; he *knew* they were kids— "just skinny teen-age girls." Learning that they hadn't even graduated from high school yet, he told them to come back after they had received their diplomas. And that is how the head of the company that became Motown met the girls who became the Supremes.

HITSVILLE BECOMES MOTOWN AND THE PRIMETTES BECOME THE SUPREMES

Berry Gordy may have looked like a kid to Diana Ross, but he was a very shrewd businessman. He began his adult life as an assembly-line worker for the Ford Motor Company, but his real love was music, and in 1955 he opened his own record store, the 3-D Record Mart. Unfortunately he didn't realize how popular rock 'n' roll was becoming; he decided to sell jazz records. The store went broke a year later. That taught him a lesson about keeping up with the music market. He then began to dream about a career as a songwriter. He started writing words and music for rock 'n' roll songs and was successful at it. Probably the most famous song recorded before he started his own company was "Lonely Teardrops," sung by Jackie Wilson and released by Brunswick Records in 1958.

It didn't take Berry Gordy long to find out that it was easy to be exploited in the music business. A publisher in New York owed him a thousand dollars and wouldn't pay him. He went to a lawyer and said he wanted to sue the publisher, but the lawyer advised against it. A mere songwriter against a publishing company? The case would be tied up in the courts for months and the legal fees alone would be more than a thousand dollars. In the end Gordy probably would have to settle out of court for about two hundred dollars. It just wasn't worth it. Berry Gordy thus learned another important lesson about the music business: If you have no control, you have no power. So he decided to become an independent producer.

He signed up his own talent, made demonstration records, and leased those records to record companies. He found his talent right there in Detroit's "Black Bottom"; he recorded a group called the Miracles and leased their material to Chess, an independent, family-run company in Chicago, and he recorded a solo performer named Marvin Gaye and leased that material to United Artists.

In 1959 Gordy's sister Anna, who was also in the music business, formed her own record label—Anna Records— and her brother soon followed suit. It is said that he borrowed several hundred dollars (six hundred to eight hundred, depending on the source of information) and with that small investment started his own record company, Hitsville, USA, an umbrella or controlling company under which were a second company, Jobete Music Co., Inc., and his various labels. He and his sister decided to work together, and the first nationally successful song they produced, "Money, That's What I Want," sung by Barrett Strong, was written by Berry Gordy and Jamie Bradford, produced by Berry's company, Jobete, and released on Anna's label.

A lot of small record companies have come out with one

hit and then fizzled, never to be heard from again. That has been especially true of small Black-owned and -operated companies, and back in 1959 Berry Gordy was taking a big chance. He knew it and was determined to make the gamble work. He had more going for him than a lot of other small-time record executives. He had already made it as a songwriter and knew the workings of the New York recording studios. His two years as an independent producer had taught him a great deal about that aspect of the business, and he had studied as much as he could the operations of the big companies to which he leased material. He was particularly interested in the workings of the Chess company, because it was family-run and independent.

The Chess staff members would listen to a singer and, if they liked him or her, offer a one-year contract with an option on a second year. Then they could polish the material, change it, do whatever they wanted with it, because in signing the contract, the singer would have signed over all "artistic direction" rights to the company. An arrangement would be made, a recording session held, and they'd have a record. Then they'd start "hawking" the record, sending out copies to disc jockeys, taking out ads in trade magazines, trying to sell it any way they could. If it sold twenty or thirty thousand copies, they'd have a "reasonable return" on their investment and would try again. The artist, meanwhile, would not have made any money, because his or her royalties of two to three cents a record would be absorbed by the company to defray the expenses of musicians, arrangers, and copyists. If the next record by the singer sold better, the company would be able to arrange guest appearances, but that would mean the company had to provide a personal manager and a booking agent, each of whom would take a percentage of the performer's profits. Only if the performer really hit it big would he or she make any money. Although the company would have initially spent quite a lot of money on launching that performer, by this point it would have recovered its investment and still have its ongoing share of the now established performer's earnings to invest in another promising new performer.

That all seemed pretty simple to Berry Gordy. The problem was in finding an individual or group that would hit it big right away, because he didn't have the money to do much experimenting. He was very lucky to find the Miracles. His relationship with that group would be one of the keys to his later success. The group's lead singer, William "Smokey" Robinson, was not just a singer but a songwriter as well and eventually wrote many of Hitsville's successful songs. But there were other talented people who helped Gordy make a success of his company. In fact, once word got around Detroit that there was a new Black record company, Gordy was swamped with talent. Detroit had no major recording company, Black or white, and the time was ripe for even a small one to take advantage of the incredible amount of talent that was growing and maturing in the city's Black neighborhoods. Within a few months after forming Hitsville, Gordy had signed up groups like the Marvelettes and the Contours and the

Primes, whose name was changed to the Temptations, and individuals like Mary Wells and a nine-year-old blind boy named Stevie Morris who later became known as Stevie Wonder. For every individual or group he put under contract, Gordy turned dozens of others away. His company was not big enough to handle all the talent that came to him, so he had to choose carefully, and early on he decided not to have anything to do with kids who were still in school. "If you were still in school, you couldn't travel around to disc jockeys promoting your records, and it was a lot simpler after you finished high school," Mary Wilson explained later. Stevie Wonder was an exception. Groups like the Primettes would just have to wait until they finished school and then audition again.

Crestfallen, Diana, Mary, Florence, and Barbara left the Hitsville studios and went home, but Diana Ross was not about to give up so easily. She found out that Martha Reeves of Martha and the Vandellas had managed to get an audition by going to work for Hitsville and singing every time Gordy passed her desk until she got him to agree to hear her and her group. Diana decided to do the same thing; maybe she could get Gordy to change his mind about making the girls wait until they had finished high school. That summer, although she could neither type nor take dictation, Diana got a part-time job as a secretarial assistant at Hitsville, and just like Martha Reeves, every time Gordy opened his inner office door, she burst into song. Unfortunately her efforts did not have a similar result; her job with Hitsville lasted just about two weeks.

But she did manage to convince Gordy to use the Primettes as background vocalists, and that was a start. The girls would have agreed to do anything short of mopping the floors to be a part of Hitsville and to be in the music business.

At least Diana and Mary and Barbara would have. Florence was not so sure. Her family still did not approve of her devoting so much time and energy to singing, and Florence herself was still seriously thinking of a nursing career. But the idea of making some money at Hitsville caused her to decide to stay with it.

Florence later recalled, "I had a music teacher who wanted me to sing what she felt was really good music, like Handel or 'Ave Maria.' She'd be talking to me about it while I'd be saying impatiently, 'I've got to get to the studio to rehearse,' and she'd say, 'What studio?' Then I'd tell her that I was singing rock 'n' roll, and she would be disgusted." Diana's parents were not very pleased either, for they still believed she was just fooling herself if she thought she had any real chance to be a successful singer.

The girls did some demonstration records for Martha and the Vandellas, and they sang backup for Marvin Gaye. They earned $2.50 apiece for each session. "That was a lot of money to us," Mary later recalled, "and we'd have to go see 'the man' to collect that too. 'Come by for our money,' we'd tell him. 'Money that's owing to us.' We used to walk to the studio, because I got so tired of asking my mother for a quarter for carfare." It would have been easier for the girls if the company had just sent them checks, but Berry Gordy wanted to be in absolute control of the company and was. A man who personally paid his backup vocalists their $2.50 a session had to know everything that was going on. That kind of control may not be advised in the various how-to-operate-your-own-successful-business books, but it was working for Berry Gordy. His company grew and prospered. He formed his own label, Tammie, soon changed it to Tamla, and in 1961 had his first hit on the new label. "Shop Around," written by Gordy and Smokey Robinson and recorded by the Miracles, reached the top of the charts, and the music world began to sit up and take notice of the fledgling record company in Detroit.

Florence and Mary and Barbara graduated from North-western High in June 1961. Diana did not graduate that June from Cass Tech. She didn't have enough credits and had to take an extra semester in order to get her diploma. She felt very bad about that, because she was holding up the rest of the group, not to mention her own career. Upon graduation they had planned to ask Gordy to put them under contract. Now they would have to wait until the following January or February.

Instead of going back to Hitsville, they had to get summer jobs. Diana went to work as a busgirl in the cafeteria at Hudson's department store, where she had long attended Saturday charm-school classes. Her job was to collect the basins of dirty dishes out front and take them back to the kitchen to be washed. It was menial work, the sort of work that Black people often ended up doing all their lives. But at Hudson's the position of busboy or busgirl had always before been held by whites while Blacks had been confined to the kitchen. Diana Ross was the first Black busgirl at Hudson's cafeteria.

As a "first," she naturally attracted attention. The other employees of Hudson's would visit the cafeteria just to see her. Being on display like that, especially carrying dirty dishes around, might have bothered other girls, but Diana, instead of resenting the situation, decided to make the most of it. "I made it a point to be beautifully groomed and to make a fine impression," she says. "Nobody would ever have anything bad to say about Diane."

Although she could cut up on occasion, Diana Ross was basically a very serious and responsible young woman. When she went back to Cass Tech that fall, her fellow students recognized that quality in her by electing her a fifth-floor hall guard, which was quite an honor. The guards had to check lockers and make sure they were secure, to make sure students going through the halls during class time had passes, and to keep loiterers and troublemakers out of the halls. The other fifth-floor hall guards honored Diana further by electing her their captain. Mrs. Aimee Kron, a French teacher, was supervisor of the fifth-floor hall guards, and she remembers Diana as a loner who did not spend time with girls other than a few close friends and who hardly ever talked about boys. She talked mostly about sewing and clothes and about singing and the Primettes.

"She had an absolutely beautiful voice," Mrs. Kron recalls. "I remember just before Christmas that year, she came into the study hall and I asked her to sing. All the students were very noisy. They were all excited about getting out for Christmas vacation. But as soon as Diana began to sing, there was almost a religious silence; it was absolute. Everyone was quiet and caught up with listening to her. I don't remember exactly what songs she sang—some Christmas carols—but they were beautiful. . . . And the applause after she finished singing was incredible. I'm not surprised that she has become so famous. Diana Ross was the kind of girl who would get what she wanted and worked hard to get it."

During the time the other Primettes were waiting for Diana to finish high school, the group changed. Barbara Martin decided to get married rather than to try for a singing career. She would remain in Detroit, have lots of children, and be very happy. That left only three Primettes, and the remaining girls decided not to find a replacement for Barbara. Instead they would be a trio. "We were used to being four, though," Mary said years later, "and for a while it bothered us to be three." Not wanting to appear as three-fourths of an old group, they changed their name. At Florence's suggestion they became the Supremes. There were times, though, when Mary and Diana wondered if, by the time they were signed by Hitsville, they would even be a trio. Says Diana, "Mary and I thought we would be a duet because Florence would skip dates even then."

36

Diana graduated from Cass Tech in January 1962 and was voted Best Dressed Girl. Now nothing stood in the group's way. They started rehearsing for a new audition at Hitsville, but before they were ready, Berry Gordy surprised them. One day when they went to him for their backup vocalists' salary, he offered them a contract. They were flabbergasted.

Mary's family was overjoyed; Florence's and Diana's families reacted differently. Although neither family made any move to prevent the girls from signing with Hitsville, neither family expected much to come of it all. Diana's father told her, "If you don't make it, don't come crying around here asking for help."

In many ways signing a contract with Berry Gordy meant signing over one's life. Gordy did not just direct the company, but the music and the music-makers as well. Anyone who represented his company, he told the girls, was going to represent it properly, and so they were required to attend daily the special courses given by his Artists Development Department. It was like a very intensive charm school. The girls were taught how to put on makeup and how to do their hair, how to walk and sit properly and to shake hands using a firm grip. By the time they "graduated" from the course, the three kids from Detroit's "Black Bottom" were as poised as Park Avenue debutantes.

Berry Gordy believed in doing things right. He considered each singer or group under contract with him as a "package" to be presented as elegantly and as professionally as possible. He spared no expense on costumes and production. Onstage his people did not just stand around and sing; they sang while going through intricately choreographed routines. Their costumes were studded with sequins, their hair—or wigs—perfectly coiffed. In those days Hitsville singers did mostly local shows, often in dingy auditoriums, but to look at them, you would have thought they were appearing at a big New York nightclub. The predominantly Black, mostly teen-age audiences appreciated the effort and so did the adult audiences at the clubs where Hitsville performers appeared. Even the Supremes' families were impressed when the girls opened at the Red Rooster, a local nightclub, and Florence's classical-music teacher came to see her student and to applaud as loudly as the rest of the audience.

By 1962, the year he put the Supremes under contract, Gordy's obsession with doing things right had begun to pay off. In that year, he produced no less than five hit records. There was "Do You Love Me?" by the Contours. The Marvelettes had two hits, "Beachwood 4–5789" and "Please Mr. Postman," and so did Mary Wells with "The One Who Really Loves You" and "You Beat Me to the Punch." Also in that year, Gordy began to use the name Motown, a contraction of Motor Town, which Black people in Detroit call the city where so many automobiles are made. At first, it was just a label name, like Anna or Tamla (both Mary Wells's hits were recorded on the Motown label, while the Marvelettes' hits were recorded on the Tamla label), but Gordy and his people liked the name Motown so much that the name of the umbrella company was changed from Hitsville, USA to Motown. Motown remains today the name of the umbrella company, under which are Jobete, the music company, and Tamla, the major label.

It was an exciting time to be part of Motown. The Supremes were proud to have been backup vocalists on some of these hit records. But of course they really wanted to have some hits of their own, and they were impatient with the Motown people for taking so much time deciding who should lead and what material they should sing, and insisting on all that charm-school stuff.

Mary Wilson had been lead singer ever since the group was formed, but that changed once the Supremes signed with Motown. Gordy did not think her voice was commercial enough. Diana seemed to him to be the one with the most personality, so he decided to try her as lead singer, but he wasn't satisfied with the recordings the group made under that arrangement. So he asked Florence to try singing lead. He was even less pleased with those recordings. Eventually, it was decided that Diana's voice was the most commercial after all, and she got to be lead singer. Mary was not even tried, and that bothered her, but she kept her thoughts to herself, believing that the success of the group was the important thing and that the Motown people knew what was commercial and what was not.

The next step was to find the right songs for the Supremes to sing. The group recorded a couple of records that first year that actually made the charts. "Your Heart Belongs to

Me" reached 95th place and the later "Let Me Go the Right Way" did a little bit better at 90th place. Considering the hundreds of records that are released each year, even to make the Top One Hundred on the charts is something to be proud of. Of course the girls wanted a Number One hit, but they knew it took time to build up a following.

Meanwhile they were having fun. They loved wearing glamorous clothes and having lots of different wigs and having audiences of kids scream when they came onstage. They loved making money. They knew it was not much compared to what a group like the Marvelettes earned, but it was still more money than they had ever had before. They all remembered that not so long ago they thought the $2.50 apiece for a recording session was big money. Florence, from a family of twelve kids, remembered being so poor that she had to go to high school with holes in her shoes, walking flat-footed so no one would notice. She remembered a time when having a telephone in the apartment was an impossible luxury; now she could afford to buy telephones for her family.

They were expected to help promote their records by making the rounds of the local radio stations and personally visiting disc jockeys to ask them to play their records. Disc jockeys could make or break a record. They were the most important ingredient in a record's success, because if a record wasn't heard no one would buy it. The Supremes enjoyed meeting the deejays whose programs they had listened to for years and didn't consider it work at all.

They also enjoyed traveling to out-of-town shows with other Motown singers in the Motor Town Revue. They would all pile into a bus or buses with their costumes and wigs and makeup cases and ride for miles. People along the road would recognize the name emblazoned on the bus and wave and scream and Diana and Mary and Florence would smile and wave back. Some of the veteran performers complained about the road trips, but the Supremes thought they were exciting. One of their most exciting experiences was going to New York with the Motor Town Revue and performing at the Apollo Theatre in Harlem. As kids growing up, they had often heard about the famed Apollo, where all the big Black stars appeared, and they had longed to be able to go there. Now, they were going to the Apollo—but to sing onstage! The first night Diana was so happy, she started laughing and couldn't stop until the Supremes were actually onstage and singing. At times like this, they all had to pinch themselves to be sure what was happening to them was real.

Most of all they were happy to be doing something they really wanted to do, and they knew they were very lucky for that reason alone. Diana once said thoughtfully, "All the kids we grew up with who got discouraged and dropped out of school because they couldn't see any future or went to work in a department store—they didn't have something they wanted to do with all their might the way we did."

Not that being under contract with Motown and not having had a big hit record was easy. They could have gotten very discouraged being around people like Martha and the Vandellas and the Marvelettes, and sometimes they did. Sometimes they thought that it would be easier to get married or go to work in a department store. "We were insecure kids," says Diana, "but Berry saw something in us, maybe that we weren't afraid of hard work. We wanted to show him. . . . We wanted to make a name, keep a name, and everything in good taste. Berry decided we had something to cultivate."

THE SUPREMES
MAKE IT BIG

By the middle of 1963 the Supremes were beginning to wonder if they were fooling themselves. Some of their records did not even make the charts, and yet all around them at Motown others were having hits. That year Martha and the Vandellas had two big hits: "Heat Wave" and "Come Get These Memories." Mary Wells's "What's Easy for Two Is Hard for One" was a hit and so was "You've Really Got a Hold on Me" by the Miracles. Even Little Stevie Wonder, thirteen years old, finally had a No. 1 record in "Fingertips," Parts I and II.

By 1963 rock 'n' roll had become increasingly dominated by albums, so the Supremes recorded *Meet the Supremes*, but that didn't go anywhere either. Everyone but them seemed to be moving up in the Motown hierarchy. Around the Motown offices and studios they were not even called the Supremes, just "the girls." There were other groups of young females under contract with the company, but whenever anyone mentioned "the girls," everyone else knew that person was referring to Diana and Mary and Florence.

The Supremes did not like the feeling of being the company losers. After three years with Motown they were ready to quit. Florence and Mary were talking about going to Chicago and joining the Navy to become Waves, and Diana, since she had not thought about anything but a career in music for years, was thinking of just going along with them. Then, their record, "A Breath Taking Guy," placed No. 75 on the charts and four months later "When the Lovelight Starts Shining Through His Eyes" actually got all the way up to No. 23. That gave them hope, and they decided to keep trying. But "Run, Run, Run," recorded in March 1964, didn't get any higher than No. 93, and they wondered again if they were ever going to be more than a minor group.

Later in 1964, when they recorded the song "Where Did Our Love Go," they didn't expect it to do any better than the others had. It did not seem too different in quality from their earlier singles. Written by Brian and Eddie Holland and Lamont Dozier, the songwriting trio that had written both hits recorded by Martha and the Vandellas in 1963, it had been arranged by bandleader Maurice King, whom Berry Gordy had hired especially to work with the Supremes. Diana sang the lead, as had become her custom. The song had a nice, smooth, but driving beat—more of a rock 'n' roll beat than their earlier songs—but the Supremes did not think the beat would make very much difference. In fact Diana later admitted, "I just didn't believe in 'Where Did Our Love Go.'"

That summer, not long after "Where Did Our Love Go" was released, the Supremes went on a bus tour of the South with Dick Clark of *American Bandstand* fame and others. They were very excited about the trip because Dick Clark's *American Bandstand* was a popular television show and all the big rock stars went on his tours. In fact, the road show was called Caravan of Stars. The Supremes didn't even care when they found out that they weren't going to make any money to speak of. In *Rock, Roll & Remember*, which he wrote with Richard Robinson, Dick Clark recalls those days: "For fourteen shows a week the star of the show got about $1,200. I think we paid Gene Pitney $1,500 a week when he was a headliner. The Supremes were on one tour, and the three girls and Diana Ross's mom, who was along as chaperon, got a total of $600 a week. Many acts didn't make more than $500 a week. . . . Once the act got paid their $500 or $600, they divided the money among themselves, took off 10% for their agent, 10% for their manager, put aside some to pay their taxes, paid for their room and board on the tour—they were lucky if they had $20 a week to play with." But Diana and the other Supremes were so pleased about being on the tour that they didn't mind the rest—until they started coming up against segregation.

Diana had not been back to the South since the time, some ten years earlier, when she and her sisters and brothers had been sent to Alabama to live with their grandparents during their mother's illness. But she quickly learned that things hadn't changed much. There were restaurants where they could not eat and motels where they could not stay because the Caravan of Stars included Blacks like the Supremes. Diana and the others had begun to feel a bit cocky about being recording artists and traveling with shows like Dick Clark's, but the experience of discrimination in the South made them lose that cockiness in a hurry. It was a strange feeling to know that the whole tour was being eyed suspiciously because they were part of it. It was even stranger to walk about a town where the white adults glared at them and then to go to an auditorium or civic center for the show and have white teen-agers scream and cheer when they came onstage.

The first time they started to sing their newest single and were greeted with all those screams and cheers, they hardly knew what to make of it. How in the world did these southern white kids know about "Where Did Our Love Go"?

"It must have been playing on the radio because people began to act like they'd heard it before and started to scream," Diana said in 1966. Ironically it was southern white kids who first let the three Black girls from Detroit know they had their hit at last. By the time they got back home, their song was No. 1.

With their tenth single the Supremes hit the top of the charts, and their lives would never be the same again. Quickly, to take advantage of their success, Motown rushed them into production of an album of the same title as the single, and long recording sessions were needed. Invitations for guest appearances poured in, and because some of them came from important places, they were reenrolled for a brushup session in the Motown charm school so they would be a credit to the company when they appeared. Diana remembers that period as the time "when we started doing the hard work—meeting disc jockeys, interviews . . . being nice to build ourselves up to pay the bills."

Before then their tours had always been bus tours. Now they started being invited to appear in cities where they had to fly to get there. Being aware of the image Motown expected of them, and thinking that flying from place to place on airplanes was just about the most exciting experience in the world, they got all dressed up in hats and gloves and matching suits; they were careful not to speak loudly or to do anything as indecorous as giggling or acting like the newcomers to flying they really were. Mrs. Ross or one of the other girls' mothers always went with them to make sure they behaved and to keep any amorous young men at a distance.

Their most exciting plane trip that year was their first tour abroad—to England, where "Where Did Our Love Go" had reached the No. 2 spot on the record charts. It was only a two-week tour, and the girls did not have much time for anything but eating, sleeping, and performing. "We all wanted to get to the London shops—we all love hats and shoes," Diana complained to a British reporter. "But we are only here until October 15, and we seem to be busy every day." They did manage to get over to the Paramount Theatre between shows one night to see the Animals, a popular British group at the time, but they did not get to see the group they wanted to see most, the Beatles. By the end of the decade the Supremes would be second only to the Beatles in numbers of records sold.

In 1964 they were still just three kids who had made it big for the first time and for whom everything about the life of an entertainer was exciting and new. They did not mind living out of a suitcase and working nonstop. They did not mind the fact that their lives were strictly controlled, even regimented, by Motown; that they were always chaperoned, that they were discouraged from dating (they were supposed to project a wholesome image, and Motown feared any hint of scandal, such as one of them dating an older man, drinking, or being at a wild party); that even the money they earned was not theirs to do with as they wanted. Although together they made $300,000 in 1964, each received an allowance of $100 a week and no more. The rest was held in trust for them until they reached the age of twenty-one and became legal adults. Berry Gordy had to approve personally Diana's purchase of a four-hundred-dollar lynx coat on the installment plan at Hudson's department store. He also approved her request that monies be set aside regularly to send her younger sister and three younger brothers to college. If they resented this control of their lives, the girls did not show it, and it is unlikely that they felt much resentment. If it hadn't been for Berry Gordy and Motown, they knew they would probably still be singing for pennies at local record hops.

"Where Did Our Love Go" was the third Motown single to reach No. 1 on the charts. It was the first Motown single to remain in the top forty songs for over a year, and sold more than two million copies. But one hit single did not make them anything special at Motown. Many Motown performers were having hit singles, and if they were not all Number One records, they were usually high in the Top Ten. Already the young record company had come to value longevity, and when it came to consistent success, Smokey Robinson and the Miracles were the group most appreciated at Motown. After them, the pecking order changed often. The Motor Town Revue shows were always arranged according to that order: The least successful performers would open the show, and the most successful would close it. Smokey Robinson always closed it with his show-stopping performance of "Shout." "A little bit softer now . . . a little bit softer now," he'd sing, getting down onto one knee, his voice barely audible. Then "A little bit louder now," in a voice getting higher and stronger until he was shouting the lyrics and leaping around the stage, and the audience was jumping around in their seats and screaming with excitement.

The other performers knew Smokey would always close the show, so there was no point in trying to displace him. But there was room for advancement under him, and there was a lot of jockeying for position. At one point, from 1962 to 1963, Little Stevie Wonder was opening the shows, followed by the Marvelettes, Mary Wells, and the Temptations. The Contours were featured right before Smokey Robinson and the Miracles came on to close the show. Then the Temptations' records started selling better than those of the Contours, so the Temptations moved up to the spot before Smokey Robinson. When Little Stevie Wonder hit it big with "Fingertips," he moved up, and the Supremes were brought in to open the show. They were lowest in the pecking order, but according to Michael Thomas of *Rolling Stone* magazine, for an ambitious and clever young woman like Diana Ross, there were advantages in that situation: "She'd sit there and watch what all the other acts did, some particular two-step reverse kick-and-swivel grandstand maneuver the Temptations might have, the way Stevie Wonder kind of half swallowed a key rhyme, any little winning trick at all—then she'd get up there in front and steal their thunder. Pretty soon she was getting down in her silver fishnets [stockings] and going, 'A little bit softer now . . . a little bit louder now. . . .'"

Diana was stealing everyone else's act, and the others were about ready to stage a revolution. To keep peace Gordy had to tell Diana to quit it and to stick to the choreography worked out especially for the Supremes, but secretly he admired her gumption. Pretty soon the Supremes moved up in the shows, and though they never displaced Smokey Robinson and the Miracles as the closing act, they immediately preceded them.

By the time they had two solid hits and another one on the way, Diana was not the only Supreme who was getting cocky. They all were. For the first time, they began to argue—about clothes, about wigs, about who was to sing lead in which songs at such-and-such a concert. But they were good enough friends to realize they were growing apart and to do something about it. They went to Gordy and said, "Look, it might be a good idea if we got together and tried to regroup. We've got three hit records now, but we're falling apart." So they took some time off and did some thinking and came to the conclusion that they were not going to let success spoil their friendship. "So we regrouped and had five more hits," says Diana.

"Where Did Our Love Go" was only the first in an astounding string of hits for the Supremes. In the twelve months after they recorded that single, the Supremes recorded five more songs that became gold records, or sold more than one million dollars worth of copies. They were: "Baby Love," which was released while they were in England on their first tour abroad; "Stop! In the Name of Love"; "Come See About Me"; "Back in My Arms Again"; and "I Hear a Symphony." They became the first group ever to have six consecutive million record sellers in the space of a single year. Because of the Supremes, Motown, the Black-owned and -operated company in Detroit, Michigan, had the biggest sales of any record company that year.

Each song featured Diana as lead singer. Her soft, sexy voice was noted by many critics, although some of them liked her voice and some did not. Each song had a smooth, polished overlay and, underneath, a blend of street and church influences. This combination came to be known first as "the Detroit sound" and soon, as "the Motown sound."

As the founder of Motown, Berry Gordy was often asked to define the Detroit sound, and so he and others at Motown sat around one day and tried to do so. "We thought of the neighborhoods we were raised in," he later explained, "and came up with a six-word definition: 'Rats, roaches, struggle, talent, guts, love.'" The Supremes were not the only ones whose records carried that sound; other Motown groups were achieving or continuing their success with it. Groups like the Temptations, Gladys Knight and the Pips, and Smokey Robinson and the Miracles had their own hits, but somehow it was the Supremes who made the difference for Motown, who managed to "cross over" to the white juvenile audience and to the adult audience too.

ON THE ROAD
OF SUCCESS

Rock 'n' roll had been on the music scene for some twelve years by 1965. Although its early influences were Black, the performers who'd made it popular had all been white. Gradually Black singers had been allowed into popular rock 'n' roll and they'd brought stronger doses of those early influences to it. By 1965 the church or gospel rhythms and the more earthy, street-type lyrics of Black rock 'n' roll records were so obvious, that white rock 'n' roll purists decided that this music wasn't true rock 'n' roll at all. That struck a lot of people as strange. After all, without Black influences there would never have been a music like rock 'n' roll, but just as soon as Black performers started making money at it, some whites decided they weren't really singing rock 'n' roll. Those whites decided to call the music the Blacks were making rhythm and blues, usually abbreviated R&B. There was nothing the Blacks could do about it, since whites controlled the music industry. (The same thing happened later on when whites in the music business decided that almost any music played or sung by Blacks had to have a separate category—soul.) In 1965 *Billboard* magazine added the R&B category to its charts, and from that time on, though white records have sometimes appeared on these charts, they have been dominated by Black records. And Motown, with its "rats-roaches-struggle-talent-guts-love" combination, has dominated Black records.

In 1972 Geoffrey Cannon, a music critic for *The Guardian*, talked about Motown's place in the recent history of pop music: "Black harmony music was first sung in church; but most of the Black groups who were successful up to the 1960s in America were owned by white businessmen who turned their singing toward comedy or novelty, on the . . . sensible notion that any sound that smacked of gospel music would be unfamiliar and unattractive to the predominantly white national audience. It took Berry Gordy, a Black man who always put business first, to break a gospel sound out from this ethnic barrier."

Back in the mid-1960s Black records were just beginning to be appreciated and bought by white teen-agers. Adults, both Black and white, still looked sideways at most rock 'n' roll, not to mention rhythm and blues. The Supremes' records were not as obviously Black as some of the other records Motown was producing. White teen-agers as well as Black could relate to the lyrics of "Stop! In the Name of Love" or "I Hear a Symphony." They had more trouble with the lyrics of a song like "High Heel Sneakers." This song was recorded by Little Stevie Wonder in 1965 and, with its references to wig-hats and high-heeled sneakers,

54

did not go over very well with white teen-agers. Motown learned that lesson quickly.

The Supremes appealed to adult audiences, too, because their sound was so smooth and polished. There was never a hint of raunchiness in their songs, something that adults didn't like in either rock 'n' roll or rhythm and blues. A good solid beat and words that offended no one were an important key to the success of the Supremes. But the girls themselves played no small part in their success. They were pretty, they were beautifully dressed, and they were very professional.

Everything they did onstage, including their movements, was very carefully planned and choreographed. A typical Supremes performance would begin with the curtain opening to reveal the three in gorgeous evening gowns. Sometimes they were all the same color, sometimes each wore a different color. Their hairstyles would be similar too—all bouffant or all French twists—but Florence's might be blond and Mary's and Diana's black. They would start off singing some of their older records, or a song or two that was a popular favorite. Diana always took the lead, introducing the songs with a joke or a brief explanation that sounded spontaneous but that was really very carefully rehearsed. While they sang, they were never still. They would go through carefully choreographed steps, moving to the right, moving to the left, doing a graceful complete turn that would have made the Rockettes jealous. Even standing still during slow numbers, they moved their hands and arms and heads in perfect unison. Midway through the act, Diana would step up the tempo and the excitement. After some quick, comic patter, she would launch them into a medley of their more recent hit songs, and just when the audience was at the peak of excitement, the group would drive them wild with a rousing rendition of their latest hit, complete with an exciting dance routine of swoops and reverse steps that would set the audience howling for more. The curtain would go down and then rise again for one or more final choruses but never enough to satisfy the audience completely, always leaving them wanting more. When the curtain came down to stay, a hush would descend over the audience, and every member would know that he or she had just had a real *experience*. Teen-agers, Black and white, envied them, and adults both liked and approved of them. Together the Supremes and their music proved to be a winning combination.

But the girls were not content merely to be successful at singing the Detroit sound. They wanted to sing in a variety of styles. They even tried writing their own music, and Berry Gordy encouraged them to do so. Unfortunately, they were not very good at it, so they talked Gordy into allowing them to sing songs written and recorded by non-Motown people, songs likes "People" and "I Am Woman."

Just before leaving for England, the Supremes had cut an album live at a Detroit club. Called *A Bit of Liverpool*, it consisted entirely of Beatles songs and songs made popular by the Dave Clark Five and other top British groups. Berry Gordy was not all that happy about doing such an album, but the Supremes now had the power to get their way in such matters. No longer were they the "losers" at Motown; they had sprung from the bottom of the pile to the top.

Their possibilities seemed limitless; together they decided to explore all of them. They agreed that they really liked performing in nightclubs, where the audience was right in front of them and they could get the immediate feedback that was missing in the recording studio. Soon after they returned from their first trip to England, they asked for and got an instrumental backup group that would travel with them wherever they went. That way they wouldn't have to rely on nightclub orchestras. Their goal was to perform at the famous Copacabana in New York.

In that year, 1965, the Supremes achieved another kind of power. They all turned twenty-one, and the monies that Motown had been holding in trust for them came under their control. They could have left Motown at that point, using the money they had accumulated to hire their own booking agents and road managers and costumers and makeup artists. Other former Motown stars had done so, including Mary Wells and Kim Weston. But those stars hadn't done so well after leaving Motown. Other stars who were still with Motown grumbled a lot about how secretive the company was about finances and contracts and wondered if the company was really paying them all their royalties and guest-appearance fees. But the Supremes never seriously thought about leaving the company; nor did they worry much about money matters. It seemed to them that a lot of money had been accumulated and held in trust for them. Besides, they all could remember when they were just three girls from the projects; they firmly believed that they owed everything to the company.

But it sure was nice to be twenty-one and able to spend some of the money they had worked so hard for. They went out and immediately bought houses for their families. The houses were all on the same street in the northwest Buena Vista district, a nicer section of Detroit's Black neighborhood than the area of the Brewster-Douglass Projects. All were simple houses, not lavish mansions. Their parents were still skeptical about their success and refused to allow the girls to spend all their money on houses.

"Money is a very powerful thing," says Diana. "It was strange, those first years when the Supremes started making money all of a sudden. I remember how wonderful it was to finally be able to buy pretty clothes. I remember buying things for my parents and giving my mother money. I tried to give my father money, too, but he wouldn't take it. He'd say, 'Diane, you save your money.' Because he knew how short-lived show business careers could be."

It isn't an exaggeration to say that in the first few months after they turned twenty-one, the Supremes went on a spending binge, treating themselves to gowns and wigs and television sets. When warned that they ought to save something for the future, they pointed to their latest No. 1 hit and declared that they could save the money that would come in from sales of that record. Berry Gordy kept quiet for as long as he could, but finally he yelled, "Stop!" He told the girls they were frittering their money away. They could not count on being on top forever, and they had better start thinking about the time when it would be all over. If they did not start being wise about money now, they would have nothing to show for all their work someday. That year, 1965, the Supremes were earning $5,000 for every personal appearance and made $250,000 apiece. (Although she was lead singer and worked harder, Diana received the same salary as Mary and Florence did.) They each received an allowance of $100 a week, just as they had before they turned twenty-one. The rest was invested by a man hired especially to look after all the Motown artists' interests.

As success piled upon success, the Supremes started looking at the world differently. In March 1966 they realized their goal of appearing at the Copacabana in New York. "You know," said Diana at that time, "we used to get excited about the Apollo. We never even thought about the Copa." They sang at their old elementary school one time and were amazed at how low the water fountains were; when they had gone to school there, the fountains had seemed rather high. They went back to the Brewster-Douglass Projects and found the neighborhood more run-down than they remembered. Even the people they remembered seemed different. They were learning what it was like to grow away from their past, something everyone does to a certain extent but something that the Supremes, with their tremendous success, were doing more suddenly than most people do.

Some people thought they were losing sight of their

roots, forgetting where they had come from. The Supremes freely admitted that they no longer performed in clubs like the Red Rooster, where they had started out. "Our price has gone up and Negro places can't afford to hire us now," said Diana in 1966. "Most Negro clubs are small; they don't know how to handle big operations. We play hotels and nightclubs across the country now and there aren't many Negroes who can afford to pay the kind of prices those places get. But no matter what color the audience is, they like the same kind of music wherever we go." But they disagreed with critics who accused them of having a "white sound." "I've never felt that," Diana would say. "I just take a look at myself and I *know* I don't have a white sound. But it *is* commercial. It's hard to describe."

Overcommercialism was another criticism the Supremes often heard. In fact, their multicolored wigs, sequin-studded gowns and perfectly choreographed movements onstage led some people to nickname the Supremes "the Extremes." Such criticism hurt the girls, of course, but it did not make them try to talk Berry Gordy and the other people at Motown into changing their sound or their act in any radical way. They were told—and they believed—that anyone who is successful comes in for a certain amount of jealousy and that it must be taken in stride. It was one of the prices of success.

There were other prices to pay. For example, they were coming into contact with people and places that were strange and new before being fully prepared for it all. For all their glitter and smoothness onstage the Supremes were still three young women from Detroit, and there were times when they felt kind of lost among sophisticated people and in foreign places. Of the three Diana was the one who saw the greatest challenge in all this. Florence was inclined to withdraw altogether; Mary tended to be what she was and to expect people to accept her on her own terms. Diana wanted to learn how to talk to the sophisticated people and how to feel comfortable in the strange places.

At one point in 1966 the Supremes actually had an entire week off, and what the three did with that time tells a lot about them. Florence rested and spent time with her family. Mary decorated the new house she had recently bought for her family. Diana went back to charm school still another time "to learn how to do things that other people have known all their lives and never think about twice. If you're used to eating with several forks and spoons, you learn which one to pick up at the right time; if you only eat with a fork, you don't know anything about when to use the others."

Such social niceties were not the only things Diana was concerned about and wanted to catch up on. She bought books on word power and studied them, feeling that she needed to have a bigger vocabulary if she was going to be able to express herself in the variety of social situations she was finding herself in. She regretted not paying more attention to her studies when she was in school. "It's funny," she said, "while we were in high school, our mothers kept telling us, 'Learn all you can, learn while

61

you've got the chance; you'll regret it later on if you don't.' But while I was in school, it never meant much to me. 'School, heck!' I'd say. I never cared. Now here I am, traveling to Europe and I don't know any language except English." Even ten years later she would still feel keenly her lack of education, find out that she knew nothing about a subject or a person that everyone else seemed to know all about, and wish for the umpteenth time that she had paid more attention to her studies.

But the major drawback to success was the lack of control the Supremes had over their own time, and to a great extent, over their own lives. They usually traveled with about twelve other people—their band, their hair-dresser, their costumer, their road manager, their driver, and their publicist. Although as a rule they got along well with these people, they did wish they could meet others. But the Motown people were so concerned with keeping up the Supremes' scandal-free image that they discouraged much dating, even after the girls had become young women. "When we're working, we don't go out very much because we don't have very much time. But we try," Diana told an interviewer for *Seventeen* magazine. "We went to Arthur's with a man from the record company and our driver, who's a very nice guy. So we had dancing partners."

Three young women in their early twenties—especially three young women as glamorous as the Supremes—should not have had to worry about dancing partners, but their traveling so much made it hard to get to know people,

62

much less keep up any kind of romantic relationship. For that matter they didn't even have time to go bowling, and that was their favorite sport. They didn't lead normal lives, and they would realize later on that they had missed something by being so successful so young.

"When the Supremes hit so fast, it got out of our hands," says Diana. "We became a piece of luggage, basically on automatic, always giving the same responses." She admits that she really can't remember a lot about those years when the Supremes were on top. Everything seemed like one big blur of bus rides and nightclubs and press interviews and strange hotels and running, always running.

→ They always seemed to be on road trips. They would be awakened early in the morning, and find themselves in strange hotel rooms and uncomfortable beds. They would have to dress and make up hurriedly but carefully, for they were the Supremes, and couldn't be seen in public unless perfectly groomed. A quick breakfast in the hotel dining room while their publicist outlined the day's schedule and their road manager tried to figure out how to fit all their luggage back into the bus. Then they would all pile into the bus and ride for several hours until they reached the next city where they were to appear. They would check into a new hotel and feel lucky if their reservations were in order (sometimes they weren't, and their road manager would have to start calling other hotels to find rooms for them). They would freshen up and head off for the local radio or television station to visit a disc jockey or give an interview and then go on to meet a newspaper reporter somewhere else. Back at the hotel they would try to get a bite to eat and a quick nap before going to the theater or hall or club to greet the crowds waiting for them and sign a few autographs. Then their hairdresser and costumer would descend on them to get them ready for their performance or performances. After their show or shows they would return to the hotel and fall into bed exhausted, dreading the long bus ride to another city the following morning.

They were always grateful when they had enough engagements in one place to enable them to stay there for a couple of days. At least they were able to sleep a little bit later in the morning—unless their publicist had lined up some early interviews for them. But they were never free to explore the city or town. They couldn't go anywhere without being recognized, without being on display and having to be charming. No wonder they argued with one another behind the scenes—they couldn't even have a bad mood in public. And there were so many problems and frustrations on a road trip. The bus would have a flat tire, and they would have to race to get to their next performance on time. Or someone would forget and leave a piece of luggage behind or misplace the musical arrangements for the next show. Or a hotel would have such hard beds, they couldn't sleep. Or a theater manager would be mean to the fans and they would have to smooth things over so the unpleasantness wouldn't reflect on them. There just never seemed to be time to do anything right.

"Have you ever spent twenty-one days on a bus, keeping

dates, keeping your wardrobe, your makeup, your wigs, singing one-nighters, longer engagements, up at six A.M. and back on that bus? . . . I've been to Europe many times, but Europe to me is just a stage door in Milan, a stage in London, a theater someplace else. We never had time to see anything, to feel where we were and what was different about it. We had no chance to make friends outside the group of maybe twelve who traveled with us."

It was not such an exciting life after all. But Diana refused to let it get her down. "It was difficult for a while. Very difficult. But I looked and saw that no one was making it difficult for me except me. But then isn't that true of all things? Don't we always make things difficult for ourselves? There I was, living out of a suitcase, always on the run and thinking it was hard. Well, it was hard, but I was making it harder, making it into some kind of tragedy when it wasn't. How could it be? I was doing what I was born to do."

A TIME OF
UNREST—FOR THE
SUPREMES AND
FOR THE COUNTRY

By the middle of 1966 the strain of success had begun to tell on all three girls, but Diana had an advantage over the others. As the lead singer, she was the star, and though the other two tried not to resent it, they could not help but be affected by it. Mary was quite open in expressing her feelings: "It's funny, since I dropped into the background, I've lost more and more self-confidence in my singing—lately I couldn't even look people in the audience in the eye. When you don't practice, you lose it. But I've been working on it and now I'm taking some leads myself—we're all sharing them—and I feel that I can do it again."

When it came to records, Diana remained the lead singer, but in live performances there was room for variety. Aware that the Supremes could not succeed if two of the three felt like also-rans, Berry Gordy agreed that the others could take the leads in some songs. Their concerts included a lot of material that did not originate at Motown. The Supremes' greatest hits were always on the program, but in between there were classics and popular ballads and show tunes and just about anything else the group wanted to do. That gave them the chance to express themselves more fully than the Holland-Dozier-Holland songs allowed, though the material they recorded was still primarily written by that songwriting trio. It had proved to be the most marketable sound for the Supremes and Berry Gordy was not about to go against the tide of success.

A lot more than not singing lead in the recording studio was bothering Florence Ballard. The quiet one of the three, she was not given to airing her feelings in public, but all the insiders at Motown knew she was having real problems, and creating problems for just about everyone else around her. Of the three, Florence was the least able to adapt to the life of a successful performer. The long road trips, the endless one-night stands, the constant living out of a suitcase really got to her. She was constantly tired. She began to drink. "It got to be too much for her," said Diana years later. "She wouldn't show up for recording sessions, she wouldn't show up for gigs. I remember one time in New Orleans Mary and I had to go onstage without her because she just didn't get there. Yes, she was drinking. But the problems were mainly in her head. She was tired; she didn't love what she was doing. She wanted out. Florence was buying a lot of furs and fancy cars, but she wasn't having fun."

Her fellow Supremes were exasperated with Florence, and Berry Gordy's patience was nearly at an end. Time and again, he warned her to shape up or she would be shipped out. She would be all right for a while, but then she would

67

go back to her destructive behavior. If she had been an individual star, she might have been able to get away with it, but she was only one in a group of three, and not the star of the three. She could be replaced, Gordy assured her. Diana and Mary remained loyal; Florence was, after all, the one who had started the group. She had always been difficult to work with, even when the group was singing at high school record-hops. The others hoped that, in time, she would work out her problems.

As 1967 began Berry Gordy made two important decisions about his top female group. One was to change the group's billing from The Supremes to Diana Ross and the Supremes. Diana had clearly emerged as the star, not just because she sang lead on the group's hit songs but also because she had the drive and the will to be the best at what she was doing. She also had that indefinable something called "star quality." She was getting offers to appear on television shows without the others; reporters were seeking interviews with her alone. Noting her emergence as an individual in the public's eyes, Berry Gordy decided to take advantage of it by headlining her.

His other decision was to replace Florence Ballard, at least temporarily. Privately he might have wanted to get rid of her altogether, but the other girls were so loyal to her that he risked making them angry if he did so. Instead he told the others that Florence would be replaced until she "got her head together." That seemed like a reasonable idea to Diana and Mary, but Florence was too proud to agree to temporary banishment. She wrote Diana and Mary a note saying that she was quitting. They begged her not to take such a final step, but Florence was past being reasoned with. In the summer of 1967 she left the group for good.

The people at Motown have always been very close-mouthed about the company's affairs. Even Motown's gold records are not officially certified because the company will not open its books to outsiders and thus will not prove that X number of copies have been sold or X number of dollars made. The company is equally secretive about such personnel changes as the departure of Florence Ballard. No one would say anything about the matter, and Florence, who had never liked being interviewed, did not change her attitude on leaving. Very soon after she left the Supremes, she married Thomas Chapman and settled down in Detroit, where her twin daughters, Nicole Renee and Michelle Denise, were born. (The Supremes had often wondered which one of them would marry first, who would have a baby first; now their questions were answered.) All Florence would say about her leaving was that some things were more important than making money and that she was just tired of traveling so much and wanted to settle down. The gossip columnists decided that Florence had quit because Diana had been given top billing, but though that may have been part of it, it was not the whole story. The real reasons were not even hinted at until nine years later, and even then the whole story was not told. Perhaps it will never be.

Cindy Birdsong was chosen to take Florence's place. A native of Camden, New Jersey, she was no newcomer to the music world. For six years she had been part of a group called Patti Labelle and the Bluebelles, which had enjoyed modest success and a couple of hit records. Not only did she know all the Supremes' songs, but she looked very much like Florence. Once, before Florence's official departure from the group, Cindy had taken her place at a Hollywood Bowl concert, and the audience had not even known the difference (which also says something about the popularity of the other two Supremes compared to that of Diana Ross). Even after the change in the group was publicly announced, it had no effect on their popularity or on their record sales. In 1967 they had four more gold records.

In those days there were few Top Ten hits that were *not* Motown records. Starting with a lone record to reach the Top Ten in 1960, the company had five in 1964, ten in 1965, twelve in 1966 and fourteen in 1967. Motown was now the largest independent record company in the world and, because it owned its own production and manufacturing facilities, one of the most independent of the independents. But Berry Gordy was not the kind of man who sat back and rested on his laurels. Although the Motown sound was so "in" that it was being copied by half the companies in the industry—for example, a company in Boston tried unsuccessfully to create a new sound called Bosstown —Gordy was quite aware that no winning formula lasts forever. He was always on the alert for signs of new trends, and he saw such a new trend in the sounds of a group out of San Francisco called Sly and the Family Stone. Sly (Sylvester Stewart) Stone had been producing records for others since 1965, but his first record for himself was the best yet. "Dance to the Music," released in 1967, blended voices and instruments in a new and exciting way. More complex in arrangement than the Motown sound, it still had the kind of thumping, driving beat that was easy to dance to. More and more of what came to be called "acid soul" was coming out of San Francisco and reaching the top of the record charts, and Berry Gordy decided that it was a sound that Motown ought to have too. Gradually more complicated arrangements were introduced into Motown records: "I Heard it Through the Grapevine" recorded by Gladys Knight and the Pips and "The Happening" by Diana Ross and the Supremes, both released in 1967, show this influence, and by 1968 it was quite clear that a change was taking place in the Motown sound, with fewer echoes of church singing and more echoes of acid soul.

These changes in American popular music probably reflected what was happening in American society, and by 1968 it was a deeply troubled society, divided over Black civil rights and the war in Vietnam. The civil rights movement can be traced back to 1954, when the Supreme Court ruled that "separate but equal" education was unconstitutional; but it did not become a really big movement involving thousands of people until the early 1960s, when civil rights workers, young and old, Black and white, began to demonstrate against segregation and to organize voter-registration drives throughout the South. Thousands of these workers were beaten and jailed, and some were even killed, but because it was a movement whose leaders were committed to nonviolence, the workers did not fight back.

71

The movement brought about the passage of several federal laws that ensured equal rights for Blacks, but a terrible price was paid in human lives and spirits. By 1966 many young Black civil-rights workers were sick of not fighting back and not at all sure they wanted to be integrated with whites who were capable of the hatred and violence that had been directed against the civil-rights demonstrators. In the spring of 1966 a leadership change occurred within the largest young people's civil rights organization, the Student Non-violent Coordinating Committee. That summer the new president of the SNCC issued a call for "Black Power." Although it was no more than a slogan, and an actual Black Power program never came about, it put into words the new militancy that many young Black people across the country were feeling, especially in cities outside the South.

The civil rights movement had not done much to better the lives of Black people in northern and western cities. Although these Black people were not segregated in the way southern Blacks had been, they, too, suffered from unemployment and underemployment, poor housing, poor education and a general lack of opportunity. By 1966 these Blacks were feeling angry and frustrated and that summer people in Watts, the Black ghetto of Los Angeles, rioted for six days. Entire city blocks were burned, thirty-five people were killed (twenty-eight of them Blacks), scores injured, and thousands arrested. By early 1967 the Reverend Dr. Martin Luther King, Jr., leader of the nonviolent civil rights movement, was warning that the Black sections in many other northern and western cities were like powder kegs and could explode in racial violence in the coming summer.

He turned out to be right. There were riots that summer in many cities, including Detroit. In fact the Detroit riots were the worst in the United States during this century. They lasted for a solid week, and for the first time in twenty-four years U.S. troops had to be called in to put an end to them. Forty-three persons were killed and over three hundred injured. Five thousand persons lost their homes as fires destroyed large parts of the city's poor Black neighborhoods. No one, not even Dr. King, could control these outpourings of frustration and anger. The federal government as well as state and local governments were spurred to action as a result of these riots and began to pass laws and start programs to give Blacks outside the South greater opportunities too.

Diana Ross was almost completely untouched by these momentous happenings. In many ways show business is another world. No matter what happens in the country, the entertainment industry goes on. Some people in show business do get involved in political and social issues, but most stay out of such things, either because they feel it is unfair to use their fame in this way or because they are not closely touched by the issues, and so do not feel strongly about them. Motown people did not get involved in these issues, primarily because Berry Gordy believed that politics and music did not mix. But even if Motown had not decided to stay out of the controversies, Diana Ross would not have gotten involved in them.

She grew up in a time when most young people did not get involved in social and political activities. She hated the discrimination she'd experienced in the South, but she didn't feel powerful enough to do anything about it. Anyway, when she got into the music world she was cushioned to some extent. Even southern teen-agers screamed when she came onstage, though their parents wouldn't let her eat in their restaurants. She experienced some bad situations: cries of "nigger!" in a southern pizza parlor; four shots fired into the front of the Motown bus. Things that made her angry had happened to her family. Once, while on a visit to Bessemer, Alabama, her younger brother Arthur was arrested and jailed for no reason and their aunt was knocked to the ground when she tried to help him. Diana's younger brother Fred had a similar experience in Detroit right after the riots. "Fred was driving my little Jaguar car," Diana recalls, "and a cop stopped him as if he had no business having such a car. The cop didn't give Fred time to explain, pulled him out, knocked him down, took him to jail, and beat him up real bad. . . . These things happen an awful lot in Detroit." Still Diana chose to deal with such experiences as things she had to take in stride. She was too busy worrying about her career to spend much time worrying about racism.

When the Detroit riots occurred, she was surprised and disturbed. She never took part in any civil rights demonstrations. "Marching and protesting has never been my movement," she once said. "Besides, I think a lot of people walk around being completely negative about the Black situation. Everything bad that happens to them, they blame it on being Black. Now a lot of the time probably they're right, and you have to learn to handle that. But some of the time it doesn't have anything to do with color. If you think the world is out to get you, it will get you, but if you think the world will treat you all right, a lot of the time it does."

Because she felt this way, Blacks who were more militant sometimes called Diana a sellout. But she was not totally uninvolved with the movement for Black equality. The assassination of the Reverend Dr. Martin Luther King, Jr., in April 1968 seemed to spur her to activity. The Southern Christian Leadership Conference, of which Dr. King had been president, mounted a Poor People's Campaign the summer after his death, and Diana gave benefit performances with other artists to aid the movement. Her efforts in behalf of President Lyndon Johnson's Youth Opportunity Program won her a citation from Vice-President Hubert Humphrey, and she believes that she makes a contribution both to increased understanding between Blacks and whites and to the hopes of young Blacks by showing that a girl from the projects in Detroit can succeed by working hard. In fact she believes that her example is worth as much as more militant support of Black causes.

Berry Gordy thought pretty much the same way. But increased militancy on the part of young Americans, both Black and white, was a fact, and he was not one to let a trend pass him by. As young white people protested against the Vietnam War, and young Black people demanded respect for the unique qualities of Black culture, he told his people to start producing songs that were more relevant, songs that not only sounded more like acid soul but that also talked about things that concerned young people. That

75

may have been one reason why the songwriting team of Holland-Dozier-Holland left Motown about that time.

The three young men who had been so productive for a decade seemed to go dry in 1968. They didn't submit a single composition that year, and in November Motown filed a four-million-dollar suit against them for failure to live up to their contract. In return, the songwriters filed a twenty-two-million-dollar suit against Motown in December. They charged that during the entire ten years they had been with Motown, they had never been allowed to study a contract they had signed either before or after the signing and that they had never understood any of the contracts they had been asked to sign. They charged that Jobete Music Co., Inc., had underpaid them royalties and had deprived them of proper accounting and legal advice. Brian Holland charged that since 1961 Berry Gordy had promised him either part ownership of Motown or one million dollars but that he'd never made good on his promise. The trio also cited Motown reports filed with the state of Michigan that detailed the company's phenomenal success between 1960 and 1968. That success, said Holland-Dozier-Holland, was due directly to their songs.

The court fight was a long and bitter one, but eventually Motown won out. Motown had managed to get an injunction preventing the team from writing for anyone else until the suit was settled, and they were forced to back down. They learned, as Berry Gordy had learned years before, that the songwriter has very little power when he comes up against a big company. Five years later, the team would return to Motown and write the kinds of social comment songs the company wanted.

The Supremes' first social-comment record, "Love Child," was released in 1968. As the title suggests, it was about out-of-wedlock pregnancy. But the words to their songs did not change greatly. Like the increase in the complexity of their song arrangements, the change was gradual and not radical. The Supremes had neither the voices nor the temperaments to be radical anyway. As to their appearance, they insisted that they had been showing that "Black is beautiful" long before that slogan became popular. But they did start wearing Afro wigs at some performances.

Other media took notice of the new consciousness on the part of Blacks. Responding to charges that not enough Blacks were on television, the networks began including more guest spots for Blacks in their shows. The Supremes benefited from this change. In January 1968 they got to play three nuns in a *Tarzan* episode. Later that year, they and the Temptations starred in their own television special. It was supposed to feature the groups rather than individuals, but it ended up starring Diana Ross. The camera singled her out more often than anyone else, and it was pretty clear to most viewers who commanded the greatest attention. Partly that was because she acted like the star of the show, but mostly it was because Berry Gordy was behind the scenes during the taping of the program and he ordered the cameramen to focus on Diana. The fact that he had a special interest in Diana Ross was also pretty clear to everyone in a position to know about such things.

DIANA LEAVES
THE SUPREMES

The skinny high school kid who had shown up at the Hitsville, USA offices years before was now a beautiful young woman. She was still very thin, but now she was described as lithe and willowy—and sexy. For all his concern with business, that fact had not escaped the attention of Berry Gordy; Diana Ross made sure it didn't. She'd had a crush on Gordy from the start, and while she continued to do what he told her, she let him know that she did not think of him as a kind of second father but as an attractive and clever man whom she admired and respected. Gradually the two were drawn to each other, and by 1968 they were, in gossip-column language, an "item."

They were with each other constantly—or as constantly as the demands of their careers would allow. On the rare occasions when they could go to an entertainment-industry party or fund-raiser, they went together, and no matter how far apart they were, they spoke to each other by telephone at least once a day. Much of their relationship was still based on the fact that Berry Gordy was a successful businessman in the music field, and Diana Ross was a talented and ambitious performer. Much of it was still based on the fact that he was a mature man, and she was still growing up. She would worry that she wasn't pretty enough, and he would say, "Don't worry about being pretty; you have character in your face." When she started to study astrology, thinking she would find out more about herself, Gordy, who didn't believe in such things, wrote her a song called, "No Matter What Sign You Are." (Diana and the Supremes recorded that song and had another hit.) She would complain that she wasn't given enough chance to be creative and to expand her career possibilities, and he would urge her not to go too fast, but he would agree to see what he could do about getting more guest spots on television and putting more variety into the group's concert programs. The Supremes began to wear costumes that stressed their individuality. The Motown tradition of a group moving completely in unison had been widely copied and was now somewhat old hat, so the choreography of the act was changed. New song material was added to give each of them, but especially Diana, a chance to display a wider vocal and emotional range. It might seem that Diana was doing more taking than giving, but in reality their relationship was quite equal in many ways: Whatever Berry did to further Diana's career also brought greater profits and satisfaction to him.

Gossip columnists and some Motown insiders—including Mary Wilson—were predicting that the two would eventually marry, but neither Berry nor Diana would add fuel to the fire of these rumors. Being more in the limelight, Diana was asked more often than Gordy about their relationship, but she was very closemouthed about it. "Marriage is a secondary consideration for me at the moment," she told a British interviewer in January 1968: "Singing comes first and will continue to for the next five years. Perhaps when I'm twenty-eight, or twenty-nine, I'll get to thinking that maybe the times are passing me by. At the moment I have a good boyfriend, but thoughts of marriage have to take second place."

Diana had decided that she could not have both a career and marriage and she had no problem deciding what she wanted more. More than anything else, she wanted to be a star, and if Berry Gordy did not approve of that decision, he never showed it publicly. At least part of him understood her completely, for she had the same kind of single-minded determination that he did, and he respected that.

Gradually, with the help of Berry Gordy, Diana Ross was placing more distance between herself and the Supremes. Florence's departure made that easier. Diana did not feel the same loyalty to Cindy Birdsong as she had to Florence. It bothered her sometimes to think that she was leaving her old friend Mary Wilson behind, but her desire to be a star overcame that concern. She knew that she had to take whatever opportunities came her way and to seek out as many others as she could, so when a chance came to appear alone on television or to sing by herself at a charity benefit, she took it without a thought. For a while, she tried to do these individual appearances in between performances with the Supremes, but that proved impossible. She became tired and irritable, and so did Mary and Cindy. The strain was just too much.

In June 1969 the Supremes were performing in a night-club in Cherry Hill, New Jersey. They arrived with all their luggage and their entourage and Diana brought along her two dogs, which she had bought to keep her company on the road. One was a Maltese poodle named Tiffany and the other was a Yorkshire terrier named L'il Bit. Every night she took the dogs with her to the club, and they stayed in the dressing room while the Supremes performed twice nightly to packed houses. Then one night Diana returned to the dressing room to find both dogs dead, and she broke down completely. The dogs' bodies were quickly taken way, but Diana couldn't bear to go back into the dressing room. In fact, she couldn't bear to stay in Cherry Hill any longer. She caught the first plane out.

The dogs had died, it turned out, because they had eaten rat poison the club's maintenance people had put around to kill field mice. But that didn't make any difference to Diana. She refused to change her mind. A whole week of the Supremes' engagement had to be canceled.

Although Diana loves animals and had cared very much about her pets, she would not ordinarily have refused to continue the engagement. She was a real trouper and had gone onstage when she was so ill that the room seemed to be spinning around her. But in June 1969 she was under so much strain that the death of her dogs was just too much for her.

It came as no surprise to Mary and Cindy when, in the

middle of 1969, Diana and Berry Gordy decided that it would soon be time for Diana Ross to leave the Supremes. A public announcement was made almost immediately, but though it was shocking in some ways—the Supremes without Diana Ross?—it did not create the kinds of headlines that it would have if there had been a lot of bitterness involved. Mary and Cindy understood that leaving was just something Diana felt she had to do at that point in her career. Her leaving would create problems for them, and there were many decisions to be made over the next few months: Would the Supremes disband altogether? If Mary and Cindy decided to keep the Supremes alive, who would replace Diana? But there was time for these decisions, for it was decided that Diana would finish out the year with the Supremes.

Over the next six months, Diana Ross and the Supremes continued professionally as they had the year before. They cut new records, appeared together at clubs and concert halls and, in December, starred with the Temptations in a second television special. Earlier that year Diana had appeared on a television special with Dinah Shore—and proved she could hold her own in comedy skits with veterans like Lucille Ball, Dan Rowan, and Dick Martin—and on several other television programs. But behind the scenes all sorts of changes were taking place, not just for the Supremes but for Motown as well.

The most important change was that Berry Gordy started moving Motown to Los Angeles, California. At first it was to be just a partial move. Gordy wanted to get into tele-

vision and motion pictures, and he realized he had to set up
an office in the motion picture capital of the world. He did
not want to move the entire organization out there because
the recording studios and all the other parts of the original
Motown record company were firmly based in Detroit.
But Gordy himself was spending a great deal of time out
in Los Angeles, setting up the new division of the company, and it was almost inevitable that Diana Ross would
move out there too. She also wanted to get into motion
pictures, and she had already been mentioned as a possibility for the starring role in a movie about the late jazz
singer Billie Holiday. In November Diana closed her apartment in Detroit, flew to Los Angeles, and started looking
for a house with a pool.

Neither Mary Wilson nor Cindy Birdsong felt the need
to move to California. For the time being, Motown's recording operations would remain in Detroit, and the two
Supremes were in the music business. They did feel it was
time to take a long, hard look at their futures. After years
of life on the road, they both thought a lot about marrying
and settling down, but they decided to postpone that for a
while. Diana's leaving would create problems for them,
true, but it could also create some opportunities. Having
decided to continue in show business, they started looking
around for a replacement for Diana. Briefly they thought
about getting Florence back, but Florence had children and
would not leave them for a second chance at fame. Other
female singers were considered, including Syreeta Wright,
a secretary at Motown who would soon become Mrs.

Stevie Wonder. But finally they decided on Jean Terrell, a native of Belzoni, Mississippi, who grew up in Chicago and whose brother, Ernie Terrell, was a heavyweight boxer. Jean and her brother had been singing together in night-clubs for about a year when the opportunity for Jean to become a Supreme came along. Naturally she took it.

Diana thought Jean Terrell was a good choice. But she also realized that the choice of her replacement meant there was no turning back for her, and there were times when the thought of being entirely on her own scared her to death. On her own, would she have the drive to succeed? She realized that a lot of the drive she'd had before was a result of competition with Mary. She'd always thought that Mary was prettier than she, and just as talented, and that had caused her to work as hard as she could to be better. "You know how a runner has somebody to push him?" she would explain. "Well, Mary and I have been pacing each other for years. Now, out on my own and without anybody to pace with, it may be a problem for me. But I think I'm grown up and can make my own pace."

She had a lot of time to think about all that during the last few months in 1969. It was a period of transition, for her and for the Supremes. Her two singing partners and Jean Terrell had to have time to work together and to per-form together, so Diana bowed out to give them the chance. But she found herself with a lot of free hours she could not seem to fill. She could spend only so much time looking for a house or shopping. She felt lonely in Los Angeles, away from family and friends. Berry Gordy spent as much time with her as he could, but since he was busy setting up his new branch of Motown, he could not be with her as often as she needed. She thought of returning to Detroit for a while, but she really didn't want to go back home so soon after she had left. Fortunately her fourteen-year-old brother, Chico, the baby of the family, decided that he would like to live in California too. He came to live with Diana, and with family around, she began to feel much better.

The old group, Diana Ross and the Supremes, did not simply fade out of sight. They went out with a bang at the Frontier Hotel in Las Vegas, Nevada, on January 14, 1970, in a show billed as a farewell performance. All the people who had helped them over the years were there—their mothers, other Motown singers like Marvin Gaye and Smokey Robinson, and show business people like Lou Rawls and Steve Allen. Ed Sullivan, who had brought the Supremes to television audiences for the first time, sent a telegram, and the president of the Frontier Hotel presented them with a plaque naming the Supremes the first entertainers to be initiated into the Frontier Hall of Fame. Then Diana and the Supremes sang together for the last time all the songs that had made them famous, from "Where Did Our Love Go" all the way through to their latest hit, "Someday We'll Be Together." As the last strains of the song faded away, the three young women left the stage sobbing, and there weren't many dry eyes out in front either. It was the end of an era, not just for the Supremes but for Motown and for the kind of popular music it stood for.

85

By March, both Diana's "Reach Out and Touch (Somebody's Hand)" and the Supremes' "Up the Ladder to the Roof" were doing well on the charts, but as the months passed, it became apparent that Diana's leaving had been a serious blow to the Supremes. The group would go through many personnel changes, and by 1977 both Cindy and Jean would be gone. Only Mary Wilson kept the original Supremes alive. They never again had a record in the Top Ten, although they did reach the Top One Hundred on occasion, and gradually the invitations to appear at big-time clubs like the Copacabana stopped coming. They had to be satisfied with the smaller-club circuit, with one-night stands in small towns, with performing in the very places that could not afford them just a couple of years earlier.

Diana, on the other hand, was besieged by offers from the top clubs. Berry Gordy had invested a lot of money in a new nightclub act for her, and it was an exciting one, presented very much like a television special. Three female vocalists called the Black Berries provided background singing backstage, two male dancers flanked her in production numbers, and designer Bob Mackie made it possible for her to change her costume onstage to reflect the change in mood of her songs. A mini-outfit became a maxi-gown; a huge Afro wig was lifted off to reveal a sleek, simple hairdo; and all the while she sang a variety of songs in a variety of styles. She would begin with a current hit like "Don't Rain on My Parade" and then move into a medley of tunes from Broadway shows like *Annie Get Your Gun* and *Mame*. Then she would talk about her years with the Supremes and sing "Stop! In the Name of Love," "My World Is Empty Without You," and "Love Child." Finally she would close the show with her own latest hit; at first it was "Reach Out and Touch (Somebody's Hand)." She did brief comedy bits, engaged in some sentimental remembering, danced—many and various things to show her versatility.

She took the act first to the Monticello Club in Framingham, Massachusetts, to try it out. Berry Gordy and a lot of other Motown bigwigs were there to see where a few minutes could be cut and where the act still needed to be polished. After this dress rehearsal Diana opened in Miami Beach, Florida, in March, and from there took her act to Las Vegas and Detroit and Reno and Los Angeles and to the Waldorf-Astoria in New York in September. Some critics complained that her act was too much glitter and too little substance: "Miss Ross is overproduced and overprotected," wrote a critic for *Variety*. "It's noticeable from the multitudinous changes of costumes, all expensive, to the changes of hairdos, to the dressing sequences onstage."

But even this critic had to admit that audiences loved the act. They also loved the pioneering atmosphere that she brought along in her first solo shows. "Good evening, and welcome to the Let's-see-if-Diana-Ross-can-make-it-on-her-own Show," she would say, and her audience would appreciate how tough it was to be on one's own and would *want* to like her act.

Diana wanted more than that. In many ways, she told

herself, she was only about six months old. A whole new life was ahead of her with a wide new range of choices. She was free to go into television and movies, even to appear on Broadway if she had the chance. The trouble was, there were many people in the entertainment business who didn't think she had the ability to be successful in these other fields and would not give her that chance.

She had received movie offers, for example, but the roles were always lightweight. She didn't want to play roles that required little or no acting ability; she wanted a good, meaty part, and she was determined to hold out until that kind of part came along. But she was sometimes afraid that it would never be offered to her. The same was true of Broadway. Broadway casting directors seemed to agree with that high school music director: her voice was nice, but it was not powerful enough for the stage.

So for the time being she decided to stick to what she knew best—singing—and she did it with great bravado. As if to show people in the music industry who thought she was taking a big chance by going solo, she recorded a song called "Ain't No Mountain High Enough." Nominated for a Grammy, the record industry's highest award, it is considered by many in the music business one of the ten best singles ever made (and by a few others as the worst). The record was from her first solo album, titled simply *Diana Ross*, although there is nothing simple about the songs or the cover.

Diana's new musical directors were none other than Nick Ashford and Valerie Simpson, who have since become recording stars in their own right. The songs they produced for her were as complex musically as the best in the popular style: lots of tracks, lots of special effects, lots of depth. The front cover showed not a glamorous queen of plastic pop, but a lonely waiflike girl; the back cover showed an evening-gowned Diana. Some people at Motown thought the cover might ruin Diana's image, but Berry Gordy believed that it was important to stress the idea of a new Diana Ross, out on her own. He ordered it displayed on a hundred-foot-high billboard on Los Angeles's Sunset Boulevard. As usual he was right. The album's first run was practically sold out before it was even issued.

Diana had complete faith in Berry Gordy. She had never even considered leaving him and Motown. Others had tired of living under Gordy's thumb, and there had been defections over the last several years. Stevie Wonder was talking about it. No longer Little Stevie Wonder, he would be twenty-one in May 1971 and free to do whatever he wanted with the vast amounts of money that were being held in trust for him. But Diana Ross depended on Gordy and was grateful to Motown for giving her a break when she was just a skinny high school kid. She had the drive and the will to become a star, but she realized that was not all that she needed.

"You've got to have direction," she explained. "I'm very lucky to have Berry, because he decides what's best for me to do. I give him total responsibility for those decisions. It makes it hard on him, I know, but he takes the time to really make sure he doesn't make a wrong decision for me.

He's had this kind of relationship with every other group, but I'm the only person that's really let him have total control. . . . I told Berry once and I still believe it, that we're a chain of two. Two links. He's the thinker and I'm the doer. If he can think of it, I'll do it."

She depended on him more than ever now that she was alone without the Supremes. She tried to act self-confident, but she was scared and lonely. In spite of her desire to be independent, she found herself going to watch the new Supremes perform, remembering how it was to be the one in the middle, remembering how it was to belong.

Diana at the beginning of her career

THE SUPREMES / *(above)* Florence Ballard, Diana Ross, and Mary Wilson *(right, top, and bottom)* Mary Wilson, Diana Ross, and Florence Ballard

Berry Gordy, Jr., founder and
president of Motown Records

Diana with former husband,
Bob Silberstein, and daughters
Rhonda, Chudney, and Tracee

Diana with Ted Ross, Nipsey Russell,
and Michael Jackson on the steps of
the New York Public Library during
the filming of *The Wiz*.

MARRIAGE AND
MOTHERHOOD

Belonging has always been very important to Diana Ross. She needs to have family around her, and it doesn't matter if it's blood family or not. One of the things she liked best about Motown was that it was a sort of family operation; many of the stars had been brought to the company by other stars. Ronnie White of the Miracles had discovered Stevie Wonder, and Stevie Wonder would marry Syreeta Wright, a former Motown secretary, in the summer of 1970. The Primes, later the Temptations, had urged the Primettes, later the Supremes, to audition for Berry Gordy. Gordy's sister Anna married Motown star Marvin Gaye. Diana's brother Fred worked his way up in Motown to become a recording engineer, and Diana herself had discovered a group of boys in Indiana, brought them to Motown, and helped produce the first Motown record by none other than the Jackson Five. But now, with part of the company in Los Angeles and part of it still back in Detroit, even the Motown family was not the same.

Chico was with her and thriving. Her older sister, Barbara, recently divorced, was coming out to L.A. with her new baby, and Diana, who had bought a house, was having three new bedrooms added on to it to make room for her expanding household. She was decorating the house herself. Back in Detroit she'd had her own apartment, which had been decorated by a professional, but it had never seemed like home to her. She had stayed in it, but she never felt as if she *lived* in it. She wanted her new house to be in *her* taste and not someone else's. But though she was happy to have her own house and her own family with her, Diana was beginning to feel the need to belong even more completely. "I'm beginning to feel it's time for me to have babies," she told an interviewer around that time. "I want babies, but I'm not quite ready to get married. I can't do one without the other. I've heard it's been done, but my mother wouldn't like that —and I must keep her respect."

Her relationship with Berry Gordy was still the subject of rumors. In fact, some people believed they were secretly married. Gordy was quite willing to prove the rumors true. "I have tried to marry her a couple of times," he admitted. "But why should she marry me when she's got me anyway? Now she's free, rich, and talented. Get married for what?"

There were a lot of reasons for Diana to get married. She just had not found the right person. She knew it was a very serious step and she did not want to make a mistake. She had seen a lot of unhappy marriages, including that of her own parents, who had separated by then. A lot of the kids

98

she had grown up with, including her own sister, were already married and divorced. She didn't want that to happen to her. When she got married, she wanted to stay married.

In February 1970 Diana met the man she would marry, under what she later described as "kind of strange circumstances." She was in a men's clothing store in Hollywood looking for a gift for a friend. Unsure of her friend's size, she looked around for a man who had approximately the same build and seeing such a man, asked if she could hold the shirt she was thinking of buying up to him for size. Laughing, he agreed to serve as a model, and soon they were both laughing and talking. It was, in Diana's words, "love at first sight."

Robert Silberstein was a native of Camden, New Jersey, Cindy Birdsong's hometown. He was just getting started in business as an actor's agent and worked under the professional name of Robert Ellis. At twenty-five he was a year younger than Diana. He was also white. But that fact didn't bother Diana very much. She had always thought that interracial dating and marriage were, as she put it, "kind of groovy." In 1969 a reporter had asked her how she felt about interracial dating and she had replied, "You're asking somebody in show business? I say, groovy. The last place we worked, I saw a beautiful family. It was a Negro guy who wasn't the most attractive thing in the world married to a white woman who wasn't attractive at all. Too fat. But they had two beautiful mixed kids who were gorgeous. They were a happy family. I say, groovy. It's not that you just *have* to be with a Black woman if you're a Black man, or a white woman, white man; it's whoever you enjoy being with as people. If you're not right for that man, whatever color, you're just not going to be with him anyhow. I don't think there should be any separation whatsoever. Then that's what the world's trying to get at, isn't it? Aren't we trying to blend and mix together as one, as God's children?"

Diana and Bob kept steady company for nearly a year, riding around on his motorcycle, spending their rare free weekends in Hawaii, driving to San Francisco on the spur of the moment. They talked about marriage, but neither wanted to rush into anything. Diana especially wasn't sure if she was really ready to settle down. But one day in the middle of January 1971 they suddenly decided to go ahead and do it. Each called a friend to act as a witness, and they all took off for Las Vegas and a quick ceremony. Diana recalls, "The next morning we told my mother, who was visiting in Los Angeles at the time. She was shocked. All of our friends were shocked because nobody believed we'd ever go through with it. After it was all over, *we* were shocked."

Berry Gordy was perhaps the most shocked of all. He'd been in love with Diana for many years and he'd hoped she would one day feel the same way about him. He had not liked her keeping company with Silberstein but had known better than to try to make her end that relationship. It would have made her even more stubbornly determined to continue it. He had been forced to wait it out. Now she'd up and married the man! Gordy's only consolation was

that he and Diana were such close business partners that
he would continue to see her regularly. He never jeopard-
ized their business relationship by telling her he thought
she'd done the wrong thing, and indeed it did not take him
long to put his personal feelings aside and concentrate on
how the marriage would affect his business.

Although publicly the people at Motown had nothing but
good things to say about the marriage—even Berry Gordy
told reporters that he hoped they would be happy—privately they were concerned about what it would do to
Diana's image. They knew that she was not prepared for
the reaction from the public—and she was not. She and her
husband did not come up against any discrimination from
their show business friends in New York and Los Angeles,
but they felt it from an awful lot of other people. The glares
and stares were a new experience for Diana. Most unsettling
of all were the constant prying questions from the fan-
magazine reporters. Even after she had been married to
Silberstein for two years, Diana was still being asked the
same questions, even by respected interviewers like Barbara
Walters. "How do you feel being married to a white Jewish
man?" asked Walters in a *Today Show* interview in 1973.
Diana grew pretty tired of answering questions like that.
Even making a point of the difference in hers and Bob's
races seemed to Diana to be a form of discrimination, and
naturally she resented being subjected to it. But she refused
to become bitter. Maybe there were a lot of racist whites in
the world, but there were also whites who were good and
kind, like her husband. Maybe there were Blacks who hated

whites and so hated her because she had married a white man, but there were also Blacks who understood that love has no color. She just wished that people would keep their negative opinions to themselves and not keep asking her about her marriage as if it were so different from anyone else's marriage.

But people *did* bring it up, *all* the time, and if coping with that situation were not hard enough, the couple had a lot of other problems as well. For one thing Diana was still trying to get used to being on her own without the Supremes. She had found that there were more intense pressures on a solo performer than on a member of a group, and of course there was the additional pressure of knowing that some show business insiders continued to be skeptical about her ability to make it on her own. In a Miami club, at her first performance after her marriage, she varied her now standard opener by saying: "Welcome to the Let's-see-if-Diana-Ross-*Silberstein*-can-make-it-on-her-own Show." Then there was the problem of her being more famous than her husband, who did not think it was at all funny when people jokingly referred to him as "Mr. Diana Ross." And as if these problems were not enough, Diana became pregnant immediately and was advised by her doctor to take it easy just when she wanted most to work, just when she was establishing herself as an individual entertainer.

Recognition seemed to be pouring in at that time. Diana was named "top female singer of 1970" by *Billboard* magazine; a reader poll conducted by England's *New Musical Express* named her "the world's most popular singer"; the

102

National Association for the Advancement of Colored People gave her its Image Award as "female entertainer of the year" for 1970. A major milestone in her solo career took place in April, when her first special, *Diana*, aired on television. It was very well received, and booking offers came in droves. Frustrated, Diana could accept only a limited number, far fewer than she would have liked. The first few months of her pregnancy were hard, and she was forced to stay home and rest as much as possible.

It was ironic. During those long, hard years on the road with the Supremes, she had longed for a vacation. Now here she was with time to relax and she didn't know what to do with herself. She tried hooking a rug, but got so bored she didn't finish it. Then she remembered how much she used to enjoy sewing in high school and bought a sewing machine. But she became tired of that almost as soon as she started. Before long, the strain of having to rest when she didn't want to combined with all the other pressures, and Diana and her husband separated after just a few months of marriage.

Even some of the nosiest fan-magazine reporters didn't know it. Diana was still making some appearances in cities across the country, and Bob had his own business to attend to, which meant he traveled, too, so it was not unusual for them to be away from each other. By the time many people became aware of the separation, Diana and Bob were back together.

They had decided that a lot of the pressures they were feeling came from outside, and that it was up to them to decide what they were going to feel and what was important to them. They loved each other, they were going to have a child, and they decided not to let anyone prevent them from being happy.

Rhonda Suzanne Silberstein was born August 31, 1971. With her huge, saucerlike eyes, she looked just like her mother, and gazing at the infant her mother decided she had made the right decision. It had been time to have a baby.

DIANA ROSS, MOVIE STAR

In 1971 Motown announced its first venture into the motion picture business: a film version of the tragic life of Billie Holiday, the late jazz singer. The announcement came as no surprise. After all, Motown had gone to Los Angeles in 1969 to set up a motion-picture operation, and there had long been talk that a movie about Billie Holiday was being considered as a possible Motown production. But the announcement of who would play the leading role was a surprise, if not an outright shock: "Diana Ross as Billie Holiday? It will never work," said just about everyone in the entertainment business.

They had good reasons for feeling that way. Billie Holiday was born out of wedlock in 1915 and spent her first few years in brothels and saloons. A man tried to rape her when she was ten. As a teen-ager, she turned to prostitution and went to jail when she refused a client. She made her debut as a singer in small Harlem nightclubs in 1931 at the age of sixteen, and by 1935 she had started to attract attention as a unique jazz singer. After touring briefly with jazz bands, she became a solo attraction in 1940 and found an enthusiastic audience for both her records and her live performances. But she never found happiness. Her last years were a pathetic struggle against heroin addiction, which eventually killed her. In June 1959, close to death, she entered a New York hospital. But she was not even allowed to die in peace. Narcotics agents entered the hospital and arrested her on her deathbed. She died on July 17, 1959, at the age of forty-four. The official cause of death was heroin addiction but as someone once said, "She died of everything."

By 1971 Billie Holiday had become a legend, and there were few people who believed that Diana Ross had either the talent or the experience to play a legend. What did she know of tragedy, this twenty-eight-year-old millionaire who had been a star since the age of eighteen? For that matter, what did she know about acting? She'd never had an acting lesson in her life.

In fact there were only two people who thought Diana could play the part: Berry Gordy and Diana herself, and even Diana wasn't too sure about it. What made her determined to do it, and do it well, was the knowledge that almost everyone expected her to fail. She'd show them, she decided.

Although Diana was just fifteen years old when Billie Holiday died and had never seen her perform, she already knew quite a lot about the singer's life. She had started trying to learn as much as she could in 1969 when she was planning to go out on her own. She had never been able to go "very deep" in her songs, and since she wanted to sing about blues and sadness, she had started reading about Billie Holiday. No one had ever put more blues and sadness into her songs than "Lady Day." Once Diana was named to play Billie Holiday in Motown's first movie, she began to study the singer's life and music intensely.

She talked to anyone she could find who had memories of the late singer. Diana was especially interested in people who had known her well and who had watched as she gave in to drug addiction. To understand drug addiction better, she sought out both experts in treating addiction and experts at being addicted. That wasn't hard to do. When Diana was in high school, she did not even know what marijuana was, and neither did her friends. But since then drugs had become widely used, not just by high school kids but by adults as well, and not only in Black neighborhoods, but in white neighborhoods too.

She studied William Dufty's biography *Lady Sings the Blues*, written with Billie Holiday (Lady Day) herself, from which the title of the Motown movie was taken, and gathered as many old newspaper clippings and magazine articles and photographs as she could find. She pinned up photographs of Billie Holiday all around her home, and studied them carefully, filing away in her mind details like the way the singer walked (Diana decided she must have had bad feet), the ever-present flask of vodka, the white gardenias she wore in her hair, her fondness for peanut brittle (there were always peanut-brittle wrappers on Holiday's dressing table), the shade of nail polish she used, even

107

the kinds of combs and brushes she used. In the course of all that study, she found that she did have a few things in common with the late singer.

Both had started traveling to make a name for themselves at an early age. Both were very close to their mothers. Both felt best when performing before an audience. The differences in their lives far outweighed the similarities, but as time went on Diana began to feel more confident in her ability to play Billie Holiday, and especially in her ability to sing the famous Holiday songs.

She put as much time into studying Holiday's singing style as she did into studying Holiday's life, but she did it in a more relaxed way. She simply played the records over and over again. Since she was pregnant with Rhonda Suzanne at the time and spending many days at home, she was able to listen to the records for hours on end. She absorbed the late singer's style not by memorizing but by osmosis—it just kind of seeped into her.

The filming of the movie began very soon after Rhonda Suzanne's birth. Richard Pryor played the role of Piano Man and Billy Dee Williams that of the man who loved her and helped her. Diana was pleased, but a little bit frightened, about playing opposite these men, who were both more experienced than she, but she found that she got along well with them, and that helped her feel more relaxed. As it turned out, the problems that occurred during the filming did not have much to do with the actors at all.

Diana caused only one problem. She did not like her wardrobe. Yes, she knew she had to wear 1930s and 1940s styles, but did the clothes have to be so tacky? She threw a tear-filled tantrum and convinced Berry Gordy to make some changes.

Most of the problems had to do with control of the artistic direction of the film. Originally Motown and Paramount Pictures were supposed to do the film together, but disagreements developed early on. The Paramount people were not pleased with Berry Gordy's selection of Diana to play the leading role. Later there were disagreements over the script, over the characters (the character Billy Dee Williams played was not a real person but a composite of men who had been part of Billie Holiday's life), over production costs (Berry Gordy insisted on recreating the 1930s and 1940s down to the last detail, and that cost a lot of money), and over the playing of certain scenes. At last Berry Gordy got tired of all the arguing. He was going to do the film the way he wanted to do it. He returned Paramount's check for two million dollars and took over complete control of the picture.

Diana did not get involved in these disagreements, and after the scene over her wardrobe she made no more trouble on the set. She was too busy doing the best she could at her own job. The singing part was not all that hard, she found. She didn't try to sound just like Billie Holiday; instead she tried to recreate the mood of the late singer, using the same phrasing, the way of dividing the melody into small groups of notes. But the acting part was tough. She had to go into herself to find emotions like hate and despair, emotions she never realized she had until she searched for them. She was amazed that she was able to call up these feelings from inside herself, but she was also pleased, because that is what it means to act.

"I didn't try to be Billie or imitate her, but applied her circumstances to my own and did what I could with them," Diana explains. "Billie faced a lot of hate in her life, and I wanted to capture how she must have felt. . . . I never disliked or hated anyone. I don't know the emotion hate that well. [But] something that was in my heart all of a sudden just bubbled out. There were many scenes where I was probably letting out a lot of feelings that had been in me all my life."

She called up from deep inside her childhood resentment over being in the middle and not getting much attention, her anger and bewilderment at the segregation she and her family had suffered in the South, at the unfair treatment of her brother by that Detroit policeman. She let out the anger she felt against the people who looked sideways at interracial couples and the frustration she had felt when she was pregnant and had to stay home just when her career as a solo performer was taking off. She made these emotions work for her in a creative way—in playing the role of Billie Holiday.

The hardest part was holding those emotions once she had come up with them, because there were so many takes of every scene. It was awfully hard to call up honest hatred or despair over and over again. In fact, Diana learned that it was awfully hard being an actress. The days were *long*. Diana had to get up at five o'clock in the morning to be

110

ready for makeup at six. Makeup and costuming would take an hour or so, and then she would have to read through the scenes that would be shot that day. Shooting would begin around eight o'clock, and sometimes by lunchtime they wouldn't even have completed a single scene. For a "printable" piece of film, everything had to be perfect: Each actor had to say the right lines the right way, make the right movements at the right time; the background scenery and the props must be in place; no background noises must intrude. Everyone had to be satisfied, and there were endless discussions about how a scene should be played.

In the opening scene, Billie is going through drug withdrawal and is thrown into a padded cell. Diana had one idea about how it should be done, and the director Sidney Furie had another. So they spent an entire day doing it both ways, and in the end Furie agreed with Diana. Diana also had ideas about the childhood scenes—where the hopscotch grid should be placed, how she should wear her socks (one up, one down). All the other actors had their own ideas, and so did the director; and the cameramen and sound men and prop people and lighting people and script people had to have their breaks and lunch hours. Sometimes Diana wondered if the shooting would ever end.

The two-hour film was in what is called "principal photography" for forty-two days, and Diana worked forty-one of them. Forty-one twelve-hour days—and she'd thought the life of a *singer* was tough! By the time a day's shooting ended—at five or six o'clock in the evening—she was exhausted from changing costumes (she went through forty-three costume changes in the course of the film), being thrown around during arrest and rape scenes (she had countless bruises and black-and-blue marks), and concentrating on communicating in endless takes and retakes the pain and despair that Billie Holiday had felt. But when the filming was over, she really believed she had done the best job she could. All she could do was wait and see what the critics and the public thought after they saw the movie.

Filming was completed at the end of February 1972, but there was a lot more work to be done on the film before it was released. Many hours of film had been shot; it had to be edited down to produce a film about two hours long. The sound tracks would have to be cut and synchronized with the picture film. The musical score had to be laid in. Multiple prints of the film had to be made. And while all this was going on, the publicity people had to come up with a huge advertising campaign to get people to want to see the film, to arrange previews for the movie critics and the press, to plan the huge premiere that would be held in New York in mid-fall.

After a brief rest Diana went back to work in nightclubs and concert halls, enjoying the chance to perform again before live audiences, where she knew right away if they liked her and if she was good. She liked to see people have a good time, to see their faces glow, and that was something she had missed very much in filming the movie.

Not long after she had completed her work on *Lady Sings the Blues* Diana found that she was pregnant again. So was the wife of Sidney Furie, the director of the movie, and they

112

had their babies the same day. Diana was not very pleased
about this second pregnancy. Although she wanted more
children, she hadn't planned on starting again so soon.
Rhonda Suzanne was only five months old. Diana had
looked forward to a full schedule of singing engagements.
Now she realized she would be able to work only a few
months before she would have to stay home and rest again.
Worst of all, because of her second pregnancy she was unable to attend the premiere of *Lady Sings the Blues*.

It was the kind of movie premiere that used to be held
in Hollywood in the old days. Everyone who was anyone
was there, arriving in long, chauffeur-driven limousines. On
the theater marquee Diana Ross's name blazed in foot-high
letters. The women were in gorgeous gowns; the press was
there in droves, interviewing the arriving stars and taking
their pictures; thousands of fans packed the sidewalks
around the theater, screaming when they caught sight of
their favorite stars. If Diana had not been pregnant, she
would have ordered a dress specially designed for that
night. As she pulled up in a long limousine the press would
have crowded around the car, trying to get their microphones in close. As she emerged the crowd would have gone
wild, and she would have stood under that blazing marquee
and smiled for the photographers and waved to the crowd
and felt as if she would burst with happiness. It was one of
the most frustrating and depressing experiences of her life to
be stuck in bed in Beverly Hills that night and not to share
the glory of *her movie* premiere.

But she couldn't take a chance and go when her baby

113

was due so soon. That day all she could think about was how the opening night audience would like the movie. She felt good about it and knew she had done her best, but she knew that even good movies can die if the public doesn't like them. When the telephone call came from New York at last, she was both eager and afraid to answer it. The voice on the other end was Berry Gordy's, and he was excited and happy.

He felt *proud*, he said. Everyone connected to the movie was proud of everything about it. Diana knew just how they all must have felt. Here she was, thousands of miles away, and she was as excited as if she had been in New York herself. But she wasn't in New York, and deep down in her heart she knew that she had missed the most important night of her life. There was only one first for everybody, and that premiere had been hers.

That night, the opening night of *Lady Sings the Blues*, Diana was sure she had made some final decisions about what was important in her life. She would continue to have a career and a family, but her family would come first. She was not going to be a stranger to her children and if she ever found that there was a major conflict between her career and her children, the career would have to go. Unfortunately it wasn't that easy. The old conflicts would come up again and again.

Tracee Joy was born early in November 1972. While she was recovering, Diana had a lot of reading to do. Reviews of *Lady Sings the Blues* were pouring in. The reviews of the movie itself were mixed. Some critics praised it. Others said

114

it was not the true story of Billie Holiday, that too much of
the tragedy was glossed over, that there were not enough
real characters from Holiday's life in it, that it was too long.
But there was hardly a review that did not praise the performance of Diana Ross.

"Diana Ross triumphs over handicaps that might well
have proved fatal," wrote one critic. "She alone is real, and
she almost makes it possible to forgive what the film does to
Billie Holiday's memory."

Wrote another: "Singing, she does a fair imitation of
Holiday's style. Acting, she does even more. Billie Holiday
personified the vulnerability, terror, and confusion of the
performer who can't hide in a crowd or in a role. Miss Ross,
in an unself-conscious, bravura performance, makes us feel
all of that."

And still another declared, "If there's any justice, Diana
Ross should be the biggest movie superstar to come along
since Barbra Streisand, and she possesses deeper acting
ability."

"DIANA ROSS *IS* BILLIE HOLIDAY" announced the
ads for the movie, and no doubt a lot of people went to see
the movie because of that. A lot of other people went for
other reasons. In spite of the mixed critical reviews *Lady
Sings the Blues* was a huge success for Berry Gordy and
Motown. It made millions, and established Motown Industries, Inc., in the movie field. When Diana Ross was nominated for an Academy Award for best actress, it looked as
if Berry Gordy might do in the movie business what he had
already done in the music business.

115

Diana hardly had time to enjoy the idea of her nomination. She was too busy preparing to open in Las Vegas in February 1973 and trying to find a combination nurse and traveling companion for the children so they could go with her. She was determined not to neglect them, and had decided that they would travel with her whenever possible. When they couldn't, she called home five times a day to see how "her babies" were doing. She was finding out that being both a star and a full-time mother was pretty hard, but she was willing to accept the responsibility. She felt calmer now, and did not get upset as often as she used to. People around her noticed a difference in her since *Lady Sings the Blues*, and Diana noticed a difference in herself. During the course of that movie she'd had to enter the life of another person, to study intensely how that other person felt and reacted to the world. In so doing, she learned how to relate to other people differently, to listen to them, to understand better how they might be feeling.

Diana and her husband were getting along well. She was enjoying family life, watching her children learn and grow. She was in great demand as a singer, and now she had proved that she was a talented actress too. On top of all this she was up for an Academy Award and had a fair chance of winning it.

The nomination for the Oscar hadn't seemed all that important to her when she'd first learned about it. But when she found out that no Black actress had ever before received the nomination for best actress, it suddenly became very important to her. "I said to myself then, I'd really like to make it, because I got to thinking, as many Black people as there are in show business, it's really kind of amazing that a Black has never won best actress, or even been a nominee." If she didn't win it, she hoped it would go to the other Black actress who had been nominated: Cicely Tyson was up for the award for her role in *Sounder*.

Neither Diana Ross nor Cicely Tyson won the Oscar. Instead, Liza Minnelli won it for her performance in *Cabaret*. A lot of insiders speculated that Diana would have won if Motown and Paramount Pictures had not tried to sell her so hard.

It is common for motion picture companies to campaign for their movies, actresses, and actors that have been nominated for Academy Awards. They take out ads in trade newspapers and the *Los Angeles Times*, and for weeks before awards night readers of these papers are treated to lots of these ads. Motown and Paramount were not alone in pushing their star; the producers of the movie *Cabaret* were advertising as much as they were. But the ads for *Cabaret* showed scenes involving the whole cast—they were pushing both the cast and the movie. The Motown-Paramount ads were only about Diana Ross. They didn't even have any words—they didn't even use her name—just lots of pictures of Diana. Far from persuading Academy voters to vote for Diana, they had the opposite effect. One anonymous Academy member told a Hollywood columnist, "Diana Ross was a runaway cinch to win the best actress award when she was first nominated. Then came those almost daily ads in the trade papers. I still think Diana gave the best performance, but the only way we can stop this horrible circus is by protest vote. That's why I voted for Liza Minnelli."

Diana read comments like this and heard industry gossip. She knew that racism comes in many disguises; she believed that some Academy members had not voted for her just because she was Black, and that the ad campaign had nothing to do with it. But she also realized that some people really did resent all the advertising and other attempts to influence their votes. For the first time in her relationship with Berry Gordy, she had a few doubts about his ability always to make the right decisions for her. But she shrugged them off. After all if it hadn't been for Gordy she would never have had the chance to play Billie Holiday. And if it hadn't been for Gordy, she would never have been the success she was. Besides, that huge ad campaign might not have cost her the Oscar for best actress. After all, Liza Minnelli had given a tremendous performance in *Cabaret*, and maybe most of the voters simply thought Liza was the better actress. She reminded herself that she had been disappointed before. *Lady* was only her first film; there would be others. She just hoped the others would have the same kind of meaning for her as *Lady* had. Making that film had been the most exciting experience of her life.

Babies and a movie had kept Diana Ross from making many stage appearances for over two years, and now that she was free to return to the stage she did so eagerly. A whole new stage show was created for her, and in September 1973 she took that show to England, where she had not appeared since 1969. She got rave reviews there. One critic wrote of her performance that "she erupted like a woman hungry to feed upon live performance, and one to whom the years had taught new artistry."

Back in the United States she spent Christmas with her husband and children in Los Angeles, then left for Lake Tahoe, Nevada, for a week of performing there, although she would have preferred to stay with the family because both Rhonda and Tracee were sick. After closing at Lake Tahoe on January 2, she boarded a plane for Detroit, where she was to sing at Mayor Coleman A. Young's inaugural concert on January 3. Somehow both her musical arrangements and her wardrobe were lost en route. Everything was in chaos. While someone ran out to buy Diana an evening gown, her conductor started writing the music from memory (the musicians practiced right up to the last minute). When the curtain went up, there stood Diana in a gown that was too big for her, unsure of her cues, yet prepared to sing unfamiliar arrangements as best she could. Not long after she started singing, someone in the audience called out, "You can do better than that."

"I'm trying hard to give you a good show," Diana answered. "I want to do it right and I wish I had all the things we usually have." She then explained about all that had gone wrong.

A little while later, another man in the audience stepped up to the stage while she was singing and reached out and took her hand. Diana held his hand until he let go, and the audience applauded them both—Diana for going on with her performance even though everything had gone wrong and the man for understanding what she was going through.

Diana was also anxious to get back to the recording studio. The only album she'd recorded in 1972 was the sound track for *Lady Sings the Blues*, and though it had done much better on the charts than her previous solo albums, she wanted to get back to doing albums of songs of her own choice. In 1973 her album *Touch Me in the Morning* was issued. The title song was also recorded as a single and soared to No. 1 on the singles charts almost immediately. Three more albums were issued in 1974: a Christmas album titled *Motown Christmas*, a sound track from one of her shows in Las Vegas called *Live at Caesar's Palace*, and *Last Time I Saw Him*. The title song of that last album also reached the top fifteen on the charts. There were more awards for "top female singer" and "female entertainer of the year," and as if all this were not enough, Diana was to star in a fashion film.

It would be Motown's second venture into motion pictures, and it was no accident that in looking around for another movie for Diana Ross, Berry Gordy had chosen a script about a fashion designer. He knew that Diana had studied fashion design in high school and had once considered a career as a designer. Still he was probably not prepared for Diana's excited reaction to the script. Not only did she want to star in the film, she also wanted to design the costumes! Here at last was her chance to use her talents as a fashion designer.

Berry Gordy didn't think that was such a good idea, but Diana has a way of stubbornly holding out when there is something she really wants, and Berry Gordy knew her well enough to know she would not back down. If he wanted her to star in the film, he would have to let her do the designing. Finally he gave in—she could design the costumes.

Now Diana added a new activity to her already busy schedule. She began to search for design ideas. Whenever she wasn't mothering or recording or performing, she was visiting Los Angeles boutiques. She found exactly what she wanted in a small Oriental shop; the multicolored paper kites on display there stuck in her mind. "I remembered these little kites and other Oriental things such as fans and trinkets, and we blew them up into something bigger, transforming them into gigantic beaded gowns and really extravagant costumes." With the help of a seamstress Diana created more than fifty costumes, working on the designs for months and personally supervising every part of their manufacture. Meanwhile she shopped for furs and accessories like scarves and belts and jewelry. It was a wonderful, exciting time, because at last she was getting the chance to do what she had dreamed about doing as a youngster, and doing what she had dreamed about doing as a teen-ager too —designing and acting both.

The filming of *Mahogany* began in November 1974. The first scenes were shot in Chicago, and during that time Berry Gordy and the director Tony Richardson had such violent disagreements that Richardson quit and Gordy decided to direct the movie himself. After filming in Chicago was completed, the whole production company and cast packed off to Rome for five weeks, and since Diana was not about to leave Rhonda and Tracee alone that long, she had to juggle the arrangements to have them join her as well as oversee the transporting of the wardrobe she had personally created. Her role in this film was a lot less demanding than her role in *Lady Sings the Blues* had been and she was grateful for that. If she'd had to work at sheer acting in *Mahogany* as much as she'd had to in *Lady*, she might not have been able to do it.

The movie is about a poor Chicago secretary named Tracy Chambers who attends fashion courses at night and dreams of being a designer or model. She falls in love with a politician named Brian Walker (played by Billy Dee Williams, Diana's costar in *Lady*), but she will not give up her

122

dream of a career in order to get married. She meets a famous fashion photographer, and his photographs of her make her famous as a model. He renames her Mahogany and falls in love with her, but he is so possessive that he cannot bear the idea of her loving someone else. He tries to kill them both by smashing up his sports car. He dies. She is rescued by a wealthy Italian who provides the money and workroom space she needs to create her fashion designs. He rents a theater for her first fashion show and invites all the famous fashion experts. They love her designs, and she has all she ever wanted—except love. In the end Mahogany gives it all up to go back to Chicago and Brian Walker.

In many ways all Diana had to do in that movie was play herself—poor young Black girl who makes it big. She did not have to "get inside" her character in the same way as she had to "get inside" Billie Holiday in order to play that role. She had wanted to do the movie because of the chance it gave her to show her talent at fashion design, but at times she wished there was more "meat" to the part. And, if she had been the director, she might have made different choices, especially about the ending. "It was a happy ending," she said, describing the way the story turned out. "At least she marries the hero. But after two years, when she's pushing baby carriages up and down, up and down, who can tell how she'll feel?"

Since Mahogany wasn't a real person, Diana Ross was clearly talking about herself. Marriage and children had complicated her life and brought a lot of added responsibility. Until then, her life had been all Diana Ross. "Then *zap*,

I had to share the bathroom. I had to learn to share everything, and it wasn't easy. It used to be my makeup, my gowns, my appointments. Now I don't get time to worry about my exercises." And it wasn't just physical things that she had to share. She had to give so much of herself, constantly stretching her ability to be understanding and sympathetic and wise, especially with her children.

Diana needs to do her absolute best in whatever she does, and child-rearing was no exception. She bought all kinds of books on the subject, seeking in them the wisdom she felt she lacked at times. At one point one of her daughters had a bed-wetting problem, which wouldn't have bothered Diana too much if the little girl had stayed in her own bed. But she liked to crawl into bed with Mommy in the mornings. The first time Diana woke up to find her bed wet, she got angry and started shouting. Her daughter wouldn't even look at her for the rest of the day, and Diana felt terrible. She looked up bed-wetting in her books and learned that one had to be very careful in handling the situation, since it wasn't right to make a child feel guilty about something that wasn't really the child's fault. The next time it happened, Diana didn't get angry.

Sometimes the responsibilities of raising two little girls and maintaining her career got to be too much for her. She was feeling that way when she talked about the ending in *Mahogany*. So it was a bad time for her to find out that she would soon have yet another responsibility. Hardly had the filming of *Mahogany* been completed than Diana discovered she was pregnant again. It seemed to her that her life was

124

being measured out in movies and babies: "I'd have a baby and then do a movie, or maybe it was do a movie, and then have a baby." Whatever the sequence, Diana was not happy to be pregnant for the third time.

Ever since her first pregnancy, Diana had wrestled with her conflicting desires for a family and a career. She had seesawed back and forth, loving her children and realizing she did not want to neglect them, but loving her career, too, and not wanting to give that up. It was as if she were a piece of Turkish taffy being pulled two different ways. She desperately needed to be loved, to be *somebody* to people. There is absolutely no somebody like a mother, and having children who depended on her and to whom she was practically the whole world made Diana feel needed and loved. But she also needed the love and attention of a large number of people—people she didn't even know. She needed the screams and the cheers and the thunderous applause that she got from nightclub audiences. The first kind of love brought her fulfillment as a woman, the second brought her fulfillment as a person and an artist. She needed both, but it was hard to have both, and her conflict was constant and unending. In experiencing this conflict, she wasn't all that different from a lot of other women who try to combine a career and motherhood. They want both, but in order to have both they have to neglect part of each, or at least that's how they feel. It's a no-win situation, and there is a lot of guilt involved.

And so whenever Diana found herself wishing her life was as simple as it used to be before she'd had children, she felt guilty. She felt so guilty about wishing she wasn't pregnant for the third time—at least not so soon—that she decided the only way to make up for her selfishness was to quit work entirely. She told Berry Gordy and Motown to cancel all her appearances. Gordy tried to talk her out of it but she refused to listen. A glum spokesman for Motown reported that the company had been forced to cancel one and a half million dollars worth of engagements because Diana had decided to stay home.

For a while Diana was glad to be at home. The last eleven months had been so busy—working on the costume designs for *Mahogany*, filming the picture, getting her new stage show ready, performing, recording—that she'd hardly had time to breathe. She felt she owed it to her husband and children to spend time with them. But pretty soon she was bored and depressed. She slept more than she needed to. She even stopped putting on makeup, which was a sure sign of depression in her. Diana Ross always feels best, even when she is all alone, when she is wearing at least some makeup. When she doesn't put on any at all, it means she isn't feeling very good about herself. She kept telling herself that she should enjoy the chance to spend time with her children, to travel with her husband (he managed Billy Preston, who was the guest pianist on the Rolling Stones' U.S. tour that year, and the whole Silberstein family went to Detroit when the Stones appeared there), and to have more time to herself. But she missed performing too much. She decided it was better to be happy and a little guilty than unhappy and free of guilt. As soon as she could, after the baby was born, she was going to resume her career.

126

Diana's and Bob's third child was born on November 11, 1975. It was another girl, and they named her Chudney Lane, a variation on the name Chutney, with the *d* for Diana. The idea of Diana Ross with three daughters struck one friend as funny. Producer Howard Rosenman sent her a note saying, "Congratulations, Diana. Now you can form your own Supremes."

Mahogany premiered about a month after Chudney was born. Diana was able to go to this premiere, but as she had expected, she did not feel the same way about this opening as she had about the premiere of *Lady Sings the Blues*. The opening of her second movie was not nearly as exciting as the premiere of her first. Unfortunately, the critics felt the same way, though not for the same reasons.

Mahogany was attacked as sexist—the heroine gave up a successful career to get married—and as having nothing whatsoever to do with the Black experience—Mahogany was Black but she could just as easily have been white. It was also called "glossy" and "unrealistic." Diana's performance wasn't panned, but it wasn't praised either, and although some critics liked her costumes, more called them far-out, "lacking in truth," a "showman's delight," rather than clothes that could actually be worn. Diana read the reviews and tried not to be upset by them. In fact, she read them to learn from them—if she thought they were honest and sincere. She understood how people could see the movie as sexist, but she disagreed with those who thought it was irrelevant to the Black experience and with those who thought her designs were "lacking in truth." But she did not become angry about it all. Nor did she regret having done the film. She had enjoyed the experience, especially the chance to design the costumes. And she made lots of money from it. In spite of the poor reviews *Mahogany* was a hit at the box office, making millions for Motown and Diana Ross. And, most important of all for a woman who had been out of the spotlight while she was having a baby, it put her name and her face before the public again.

The name of another former Supreme came into the spotlight in early 1976, but the circumstances were tragic ones. Florence Ballard died in February at the age of thirty-two. Officially the cause was cardiac arrest, but those who knew her well knew that she had died of unhappiness as much as anything else. She and her husband had broken up and she had been left with three children to support. Desperate for money, she had filed suit against Motown and the Supremes in 1971, charging that she was still owed eight million dollars in royalties. She said she had received no royalties whatsoever from Motown since she had left the group. Motown insisted that it had made a large cash settlement with Florence when she left and that in return she had relinquished all claims on the Supremes and their earnings. Florence lost the suit. She was on welfare the year before she died; she was also on the bottle.

Diana found it hard to understand what had happened to Florence. She knew that people could get so depressed and desperate that they just gave up. In a way Billie Holiday had done that. But Billie Holiday had not had as many chances as Florence had. For the life of her Diana could not understand how Florence had allowed herself to get so low, and when speaking of Florence's death, she could not help the note of impatience that crept into her voice. "Florence was always on a totally negative trip. She wanted to be a victim. Then when she left the Supremes and the money stopped coming in, it really messed up her head. She couldn't even afford to take care of her kids toward the end."

Diana remembered that her father had once warned her to save her money. When the Supremes had first started making real money, she had wanted to give him some, and he had refused. Her father and her mother had been separated for some years, but Diana still went to him for advice sometimes, because he had always given her good counsel. "He knew that it's a lot easier to go from having no money to having a lot than it is to go from being rich to being poor," Diana recalls. "That's what messes up your head, having it and then not having it. That's what happened to Florence."

In spite of her inability to understand how Florence could let herself go down, Diana had tried to help. So had Berry Gordy and Mary Wilson. But Florence had been a proud woman and had refused all help. "She was in a strange position," Diana explains. "She felt that anyone who wanted to do anything for her was doing it out of guilt, and she made everyone around her suffer. . . . If

130

I'd known how it was going to end with Florence, maybe I would have taken more time with her. But when you're around somebody as negative as Florence, it just brings you down, too, and so I quit trying. Maybe I should have slapped her face a few times, tried to knock some sense into her."

The saddest part was that just before her death Florence had started to get hold of herself. About a month before, Florence had called Diana and told her she realized that she had only herself to blame for the predicament she was in. Diana had been very relieved to hear that and hopeful that Florence would be able to straighten herself out. But it had all come too late, and that angered Diana. What a waste of a life, she thought.

Diana went through a range of emotions as a result of Florence's death. First she felt guilty for not doing more to help her friend. Then she felt angry at Florence: she'd had it all and had thrown it away; she'd quit the Supremes, they hadn't quit her. She'd brought it all on herself. And finally, Diana just felt sad, and in a quiet way she went about paying her respects to her childhood friend. She attended the funeral—most of the Motown executives, including Berry Gordy, did not—and after the funeral she set up a trust fund for Florence's three children. She did it without trying to publicize the gesture, and it did not get a lot of publicity, for which she was grateful. She didn't want to talk about Florence's death any more than she absolutely had to.

But she thought about it a lot, thought about how she

and Florence had grown up in Detroit's "Black Bottom," how both had somehow managed to develop talent and class, how their lives had been so different since then. She would get angry and sad all over again, and finally she hardened herself against these feelings and decided not to think about Florence anymore because it hurt too much. She decided not to talk about Florence anymore either. "Florence was very important in my life, but I'm not dead," she told a *People* magazine interviewer at the end of March. "She did this to herself."

In a way Diana had lost a part of her own past with the death of Florence, and that scared her a little. To blot out her fears she plunged into her work to show the world, and especially herself, that Diana Ross was a winner, not a loser like Florence Ballard. Taking advantage of the publicity she received because of *Mahogany*, she recorded a new album which was released in April 1976. Called simply *Diana Ross*, just like her first solo album, it contained several songs that could be released as singles. Hal Davis, who had produced the album for Motown, thought a cut called "Love Hangover" was ideal for such release. It started out as a ballad and wound up as a disco song, and Davis thought that was a winning combination. But other people at Motown had different ideas. "I Thought It Took a Little Time (But Today I Fell in Love)" was released as the single from the album instead, and the single-edited version of "Love Hangover" remained in the Motown vaults.

Meanwhile, over at ABC Records, the producer of the

Fifth Dimension had been waiting to see which song Motown would release as a single. When he found out it wasn't "Love Hangover," he quickly got the Fifth Dimension to record and release it. That got Motown angry, and two days later Diana's recording of the song was released. It might have been an interesting race if the sides had been more evenly matched, but the Fifth Dimension was a group still struggling to find itself after the departure of Marilyn McCoo and Billy Davis, and Diana Ross was . . . Diana Ross. By June her recording was the No. 1 single on the charts, making Diana, as a solo star, the first woman to have four songs top those charts.

No sooner had *Diana Ross* been completed than Diana began work on another album. She was thirty-one years old now, and her voice had matured. She had lived enough to be able to put some experience into the blues songs she liked to sing. She also enjoyed singing soft ballads and popular songs, and she still liked to sing her earlier hits. That meant cutting a lot of records. That year, in fact, she issued four albums: *Diana Ross, Greatest Hits, Disc-o-Tech Vol.4*, and *An Evening with Diana Ross*.

She also carried a full schedule of live performing engagements and had a brand-new act that was even more complex and costly than her earlier solo club-presentations. The overture to the act began with her No. 1 hit, the theme from *Mahogany* ("Do You Know Where You're Going To"), and Diana entered in a white, flared gown. Soon she was joined by two mimes, one Black wearing black makeup and one white wearing white. She then opened out her wide white skirt to form a movie screen on which were projected images of her, singing. She sang Burt Bacharach songs and her own hits, "Touch Me in the Morning," and "Love Hangover." In the second act she sang some Billie Holliday songs and a medley of Supremes' hits, telling the story of her rise to stardom from the Detroit projects. She finished with a rousing rendition of "Reach Out and Touch (Somebody's Hand)." In between, there was dancing and comedy skits and patter with the audience. It was a full two hours long, and almost all Diana Ross.

As usual some critics thought that the show was overproduced and that Diana was overpackaged. But by now more critics were willing to view her act as the audience did and to see it as a cross between Broadway theater and pop music. She took the show to Europe and got similar mixed reactions from the critics there. "Whatever Diana Ross is concerned with these days, music comes seemingly low on the list," wrote a critic in *Melody Maker*. But in Europe, as in the United States, the audiences loved the evening. The same *Melody Maker* critic wrote about the enthusiastic audience response to Diana's singing of "Reach Out and Touch (Somebody's Hand)": "A lady in one of the boxes high up at the side of the hall was so enthusiastic that she jumped up and down, beating her hands on the balcony so hard that she came clean out of her low-cut evening dress."

Diana was in Amsterdam in late March when the annual Academy Awards were presented. "Do You Know Where

You're Going To" was up for the best song award. Since the ceremonies' producer wanted Diana to sing it, no matter where she was, she became the first performer to take part in the annual Oscar award ceremony by remote broadcast from Europe. (Nonetheless the song didn't win.) There were also television appearances and lots of scripts to read for possible new movie projects and maybe even a role in a Broadway play. She welcomed it all. Gone were the conflicts she had felt about trying to have a career and to be a wife and mother too. Or at least most of the conflicts were gone. She still wished she could spend more time with her children, but she did not feel guilty about her career anymore, especially since she had come to believe that her love for entertaining was not selfish.

She had come to this conclusion as a result of est. The letters stand for Erhard Seminars Training, and a man named Werner Erhard started it all. He decided that people are unhappy, or frightened, or shy because they are thinking of themselves in a negative way. At est seminars people learn how to think of themselves positively. They are taught that they bring a lot of unhappiness on themselves, that how they act makes a big difference in how they are treated. Diana often wished Florence had gone to some est meetings. Despite the fact that many people feel that est is over-simplistic and a fraud, Diana believes in est. After her est courses she was known to remind herself in odd ways of what she'd learned. During an engagement at Caesar's Palace in Las Vegas, she scrawled with a bar of soap on her dressing-room mirror, "You can have it any

135

way you want it" (which, oddly enough, is exactly what her parents used to tell her as a child).

Sometimes the est seminars may produce results that are not what the participants expect. Diana and Bob went to est seminars together. Diana learned that she should not feel guilty about wanting a career and a family, that her happiness was up to her. Bob, it seems, learned that he should not feel guilty about wanting Diana to stay home more. Both learned to understand each other better, but neither could handle what they came to understand. By June 1976 they had decided that both of them would be unhappy if they stayed married.

That month, Diana took her act to Broadway for the first time, opening at the Palace Theatre. She took her children with her, and it was in New York that her manager announced officially that Diana and Bob were divorcing after five years of marriage.

The divorce had not come about because of racial differences. Although the first year or two had been hard, Diana and Bob had come to understand that there were a lot of people in the world with small minds and they could not allow those people to affect their relationship. It had come about for many of the same reasons that other couples divorce—there just wasn't enough room in the marriage for both of them to grow and to be happy. Their ideas of what marriage was supposed to be like were not the same. Diana wanted more freedom than Bob was willing to allow his wife to have. He wanted more time and attention than she was willing to give.

In addition Bob resented the influence that Berry Gordy had with Diana. All during the marriage, Gordy had been a frequent visitor in the Silberstein home and had even gone along on family vacations. Bob had gotten tired of that. He also thought Gordy had made some mistakes in directing Diana's career. "My wife *belongs* to that company," he once said. "She's totally dominated by a man who never read a book in his life. I just can't stand it anymore to hear them calling Stevie Wonder a genius. What happened to Freud?"

At last Bob and Diana had agreed that the best thing to do was to stop being married. They parted with very little bitterness and were able to remain friends. In fact, they still loved each other, but as Billy Dee Williams, Diana's costar in both her movies, explained, "Sometimes, sadly, even those who do love each other miss and have to move on." On Mother's Day 1976, shortly before their impending divorce was announced, Bob gave Diana a butterfly pin because, he told her, butterflies were free, just like she was.

The divorce became final in March 1977 and Diana received custody of the children. She was relieved to be free of an unhappy marriage, but at the same time she was frightened of being alone, and a single parent besides. Still, she had no intention of rushing into another marriage. If she ever got married again, she decided, it would be for keeps.

It did not take long for the rumors about Diana and Berry Gordy to start up again. After all, they had been together off and on for fifteen years now; Diana was free again; wasn't it high time for them to get married? But, though a new period in Diana's life began, the relationship she and Gordy had enjoyed for years went on just as before.

Shortly before the divorce announcement Diana showed how solid her relationship with Gordy was by signing a new, seven-year, multimillion-dollar contract with Motown. Not long after the announcement of the divorce, Berry Gordy showed how much he cared about Diana's career when Motown Records proclaimed the month of July "Diana Ross Month" and began a national promotional campaign to coincide with the release of her new album, *Diana Ross' Greatest Hits*, the rerelease of both her films, and the single recording of "One Love in My Lifetime," a cut from the new album. It was probably no accident that this particular song was chosen to be issued as a single so soon after the divorce announcement. Nor was it an accident that Gordy decided to launch this national campaign for Diana at a time when she was feeling lonely and depressed. Berry Gordy was, first and foremost, a businessman, and he would never have spent all that money and effort just to make Diana feel better. But if he could do something nice for her that was also good business, he was eager to do it.

The Diana Ross Month campaign turned out to be very good business. One would think that a star like Diana Ross doesn't need this kind of promotion. After all she is already a success. But there are many stars in the entertainment industry, and no matter how big, a star can almost never get too much exposure. And so, thousands more bought her albums and went to see *Lady Sings the Blues* and *Mahogany* in their second runs at theaters, and Diana played to more packed houses in major clubs and theaters across the country. In March 1977 Diana starred in another TV special, *An Evening With Diana Ross*. Ninety minutes long, it featured Diana (there were no guest stars) singing, dancing, doing comedy skits, and paying tribute, in one segment, to three late Black female entertainers: Bessie Smith, Ethel Waters, and Josephine Baker. It took hours for her makeup man to get her to look like each of these three great singers, hours more for Diana to learn their singing styles, but she was pleased with that segment of the show and happy to be able to honor the three women in that way. She often says that if it had not been for women like these, she could never have made it in show business.

They had paved the way in a time when the odds were much greater than any she had ever faced.

Maybe it was studying the lives of these courageous women that led Diana to go against some professional odds herself, or maybe it was just her determination to do whatever it was she wanted to do. Months before her TV special aired Diana had announced that she was going to do something that sounded more impossible than her playing the role of Billie Holiday. She was going to play Dorothy in the movie version of *The Wiz*.

This movie would be yet another version of the book *The Wonderful Wizard of Oz*, written by L. Frank Baum back in 1900 and made into a movie starring Judy Garland in 1939. That movie is still shown in revival houses, and at least once a year it appears on television. The story is as well-known to Americans of all ages as *Peter Pan* is. In the mid-1970s a stage version with an all-Black cast starring Stephanie Mills opened on Broadway. Called *The Wiz*, the Broadway show was so successful that executives at Universal Pictures in Hollywood started talking about making a movie version that would probably also star Stephanie Mills. Motown contacted Universal and said it would be interested in collaborating on that project.

Diana heard about *The Wiz* being made into a movie and that Motown was involved in it, but she didn't think much about it until she happened to run into Ted Ross during a visit to New York. Ross was playing the Cowardly Lion in the Broadway show and wanted very much to repeat the role in the movie. He thought the movie was

140

a great idea and was excited about the chance to be in it.

That got Diana thinking. In fact that night she couldn't sleep because of the thoughts that were spinning around in her head. She got up and played the videotape of the 1939 film, which she had bought for her daughters, and by the time it was over she knew she had to play the part of Dorothy. At about four thirty in the morning, she called Berry Gordy to tell him so.

"Have you been drinking?" Gordy asked. He could not believe that she wanted to play Dorothy. She was too old. But the story is ageless, Diana insisted. Gordy grunted and said he'd talk to her about it another time.

When Diana has her mind set on something, she goes after it. But she doesn't just say, "I want it, and that's that." She gives reasons. This case was no exception. She bought a copy of *The Annotated Oz* and underlined it as she read. She found that the author had never said how old Dorothy was, and that made her more sure than ever that the story could be about anyone. The story was not just about Kansas or a teen-age girl, it was about finding oneself, and so it could be anyone's story. Anyway, she reminded Gordy, a grown-up Mary Martin had played Peter Pan, and Peter Pan was a boy besides. It was right for her career, she insisted, and finally Gordy gave in.

The announcement that thirty-two-year-old Diana Ross would play the part of Dorothy caused quite a stir. Many Black critics complained that Stephanie Mills should have been given the role. Both Black and white critics said that Diana was much too old to play Dorothy, that she was

141

spoiled and too used to getting whatever she wanted. The film's director agreed. When John Badham learned that he was going to have to work with a thirty-two-year-old Dorothy, he quit. He was replaced by Sidney Lumet.

Diana already knew what it was like to be panned by critics even before filming began. She'd had that experience after it was announced that she would play Billie Holiday in *Lady Sings the Blues*. But *Lady* had not been judged a flop before shooting began. *The Wiz* was. Many people could not imagine an urban *Wizard of Oz*, which is what the movie of *The Wiz* was going to be.

In the Motown version, Dorothy is a twenty-four-year-old kindergarten teacher in Harlem who is so shy that she has never been to downtown New York. One winter day she goes out with her dog, Toto, to empty the trash, gets lost in a blizzard, and suddenly finds herself in the fantasy Land of Oz, which is really downtown New York City. She finds the Scarecrow, played by Michael Jackson of the Jacksons, hanging from a television antenna, where he has been placed by a gang of tough city crows, and the Tin Man, played by comedian Nipsey Russell, abandoned in an old amusement park. The Cowardly Lion, played by Ted Ross, comes out of one of the stone lions in front of the New York Public Library. The Wiz himself, played by Richard Pryor, is a corrupt politician from New Jersey who has found a new hustle. The basic outlines of the original story remain the same, but back in late 1976 it was hard for most people to imagine how they could be kept or how the beloved classic could be changed so much without being destroyed.

142

The widespread criticism shocked Diana, and she found herself feeling very defensive. But she was no stranger to controversy, and as in the past the criticism only made her more determined than ever to prove her critics wrong. She remained convinced that starring in *The Wiz* was the right thing for her to do, not just for her career but for herself. As she explained at the time, "There's a part of my teen-age years that I missed, because everybody was in school, and after I graduated from school, I didn't go to college; I went out on the road and started working, and there's a whole area, that fun area of your life, that I haven't experienced yet. I think I'll get a chance to go through that during the filming of *The Wiz*."

The Wiz would take months to film, and Motown did not want the record-buying public to forget about its star during that time, so in the late spring and early summer of 1977 Diana recorded two albums simultaneously. Every afternoon she would go to a Los Angeles studio that Motown had leased to work on *All Night Lover* and every evening she would go to the Motown studios to record a disco album. She didn't care which album was released first and trusted Motown to read the market correctly and issue whichever album seemed right at the time.

Also, because the filming of the movie would take so long, Diana decided to move to New York so she could have her children with her. In the summer of 1977, after completing the two albums, she went to New York and rented a suite at the Carlyle Hotel for an indefinite period. She had visited the city many times but had never actually lived there before. Most of her friends and all of her family

143

lived elsewhere. She'd sent her daughters away for the summer, so even they weren't with her. "I sat in my empty apartment and looked out at the cars and people," she remembers. "If I'd had time to think about it, it would have been very scary. Luckily I was busy working."

Rehearsals started in early August and the actual filming began in October. *The Wiz* not only took months to shoot, it cost millions of dollars. There were all kinds of special effects and tricky camera work, hundreds of dancers and hundreds more costumes designed especially for the film by famous designers (Diana didn't get to wear any of the fantastic costumes, since Dorothy wears a simple dress). The flying monkeys ride on motorcycles; Munchkinland is a huge playground covered with graffiti that come to life in the form of Munchkins, all equipped with skateboards and Hula-Hoops; the Wiz broadcasts from a giant signal system atop the twin towers of the World Trade Center. Director Sidney Lumet had very definite ideas about how each scene should be played, and there were hours of takes and retakes for many of them. But he was very pleased with Diana. He called her "explosive" and "stunning."

Diana did all her own stuntwork and suffered a few minor injuries. She went about playing her role with so much intensity that she collapsed into bed exhausted every night. When the filming was over at last, she believed she had done a good job, and she'd had a lot of fun in the process, but she would not *know* whether or not she had done well until the film was ready for the public, and that was months away. Still she was pretty sure she would not be sorry. "I don't know why it was so important for me to play Dorothy," she says. "But it was, and I'm sticking to that instinct. I still think it's right."

Diana did not return to California to live after the filming of *The Wiz* was completed. Instead she put her California home up for sale and started looking for a cooperative apartment in New York. She liked the city. Rhonda and Tracee were in school there and had new friends, and though it was still scary at times, Diana liked the idea of being entirely on her own, completely away from Motown and Berry Gordy for the first time in many years. "I've wanted this freedom of space for so long," she said. "I feel like Dorothy. Suddenly *boom*, I'm in a whole new world." She had no intention of leaving Motown, or of ending her close friendship with Gordy, but she needed to be physically apart from both the company and its boss. She bought a co-op in the Sherry Netherland Hotel and, with the help of the famous decorator Angelo Donghia, went about making it her home.

Although she would have preferred to decorate the apartment herself, she just didn't have the time, what with her children and her career. She was rehearsing another new nightclub act, and plans were in the works for a new album. She also decided to hire an outside agent to represent her. Always before she had been represented by Motown, and she still wanted the company to book her club appearances and other musical engagements. But she wanted to do more films, not just with Motown but with

145

other studios, and she felt she had to have an outside agent for that. She chose Sue Mengers, the most successful agent in Hollywood, who also represented such stars as Cher, Nick Nolte, and Ryan O'Neal. In no time at all Mengers had arranged for Diana to do a movie called *Body Guard* with Ryan O'Neal and another movie, *Tough Customer*, about the life of the gangster Dutch Schultz, in which Diana would play a Harlem numbers-runner.

Not that Diana had any intention of quitting her career as a singer. Singing, putting her feelings into music, had always been her first love, and she recorded three albums in 1978. But only one of them, *Ross*, even made the Top Two Hundred list, and none of her singles made the Top One Hundred. That frightened her. Maybe she had taken one risk too many by establishing more independence from Motown, by moving to New York and hiring her own agent. Maybe she'd lost her ability to reach the listening audience. Critical reaction to *The Wiz* certainly didn't make her feel any better.

The Wiz premiered in New York on October 24, 1978. There was a great air of excitement surrounding the opening, for *The Wiz* was the most expensive all-Black movie ever produced, the first Black spectacular, and the most expensive musical ever. There was also some worry on the part of all those who had a financial stake in the movie. Would the film be a box-office smash and earn back the money spent on it? In the face of this hard business question, what the critics thought of the movie was not all that important. After all, they had disliked *Mahogany*, but

146

it had been a success just the same. But no one was quite prepared for the ferocity of the critical reaction. Although a few critics liked it, most panned the movie and Diana's performance unmercifully. *The Wiz* was a critical disaster.

Moviegoers decided to make up their own minds. According to *Sepia* magazine, the film made over a million dollars in its first weekend of selected showings in various parts of the United States, and when it began regular runs in theaters millions more poured in. The fact that Michael Jackson and Richard Pryor and Lena Horne were in the cast helped a lot, but mostly the audiences wanted to see Diana Ross—in any role.

Still, the criticism of the professionals was painful for Diana to read and hear, and it was painful, too, to watch her album, *Ross*, do so poorly in the charts. By the second week in January 1979, it had dropped off the charts entirely, and that was hard for the singer of "Love Hangover" and the theme from *Mahogany* ("Do You Know Where You're Going To") to take. Maybe it was time for a change in her singing style too.

Her new album, *The Boss*, was released in the late spring of 1979. It had what a critic for *The New York Times* called "a buoyancy and freshness that hasn't always defined her records." Even the cover of the album was different. Instead of a perfectly coiffed, dressed-to-the-nines, super-glamorous Diana, it showed a natural Diana, her hair hanging loose, wearing a simple blouse, before a background of trees. The *Times* critic thought she looked more "human" on this cover. Record-buyers may have responded to that picture in the same way, for the album climbed steadily on the charts from No. 150 on June 9 to No. 55 on June 30, and by July 28 it was all the way up to No. 31. Also by the end of July, the single "The Boss" was No. 19 on the rhythm-and-blues charts and No. 64 on the overall chart. Diana had not had either a single or an album in the Top One Hundred since 1977, when the album *Baby It's Me*, and the single "Gettin' Ready for Love" had both placed in the Top Thirty. It was a wonderful feeling to be in the Top One Hundred again, and to know that yet another big risk had paid off.

Diana Ross has probably taken more chances than any other superstar in the history of show business. As a young pop singer with no acting experience, she took on the role of one of the most tragic and beloved figures in American music history, and did a superb job. As a top Black star who had managed to cross over and attract white audiences as well, she risked losing much of her audience, both white and Black, by marrying a white man, but she did not lose her fans. As a thirty-two-year-old woman, she decided to play a role that had always been played by a teen-ager, and thousands were going to see it. And finally, after some fifteen years of allowing Berry Gordy and Motown to run her career entirely, she had begun to establish her independence and make her own decisions, and so far that was paying off too.

She has suffered a lot of pain in the process. Professionally she must deal with those people who resent her for not being what they think she ought to be. Throughout her

148

career she has heard criticism that she isn't quite real. People look at her wigs and her costumes and her false eyelashes and call her "the Princess of Plastic Pop" and "the Last of the Black White Girls." She doesn't feel that these criticisms are valid. She believes that audiences want fantasy and glamor, and she doesn't see that it has anything to do with race. She especially dislikes the image that some people paint of her as a packaged, totally manipulated star. She may have followed the advice of Motown and Berry Gordy and various personal managers over the years, but since leaving the Supremes and going solo, she has had a great deal of say in the' decisions that have affected her career. In the last few years she has insisted on, and gotten, a lot of things that Motown and Gordy have counseled against. Most often she's been proved right. Now that she has separated herself from Motown and Gordy by an entire continent, she feels even more independent and free to be her own woman.

But she has managed to win her independence and freedom without burning her bridges. On the professional level she maintains a close relationship with Gordy and Motown. On the personal level she is as close to her family as ever. Her brothers and sisters visit often. Her mother takes care of Rhonda and Tracee and Chudney whenever she is on the road or on tour abroad. "I'm actually a copy of my mother," says Diana, "because everything she taught me—that's the way I raise my children. I hear myself talking to my kids and I sound just like her. So really, when she's there with them, she says the same things I do."

Diana is good friends with her former husband, Bob Silberstein. He moved to New York sometime after Diana did, and he visits the children often.

Nor has Diana forgotten about Detroit. She still visits her family there. Sometimes, she even goes to Hudson's department store where, the summer after her senior year in high school, she was the first Black busgirl. She still recognizes some of the sales people, and they are excited and pleased that Diana Ross actually remembers who they are. She is secure enough in who she is not to have to pretend that she doesn't remember where she came from. "I remember that girl very clearly," she says, speaking of herself before her stardom. "The source of my life has not changed really that much. My ambitions are the same, my caring about people and love for children are the same. Lots of that hasn't changed in me."

To have gained the adoration of millions without having to give up the love of those who "knew you when" is no small task for a superstar. But Diana Ross has done it, as she has managed to do just about everything else she has set her mind to do. She still has fears, fears of "messing up" and not being good and not having people like her. It is very important to Diana—independent as she is and controversial as she has been—that people like her, even love her, when she is onstage. And she would like to have the kind of personal love she has not had since her divorce from Robert Silberstein. "I had a lovely marriage," she says. "When you find someone that you can enjoy a lot of the same pleasures with—even if it's sitting in front of the television late at night with a big sandwich—it's terrific." She also misses the idea of the whole family unit—father, mother, and children all enjoying each other and fighting with each other and somehow making it all work together. Her own parents did not separate until Diana was grown and had left home, and she wishes her own three daughters could have the same family experience she had. But though she would like to get married again, Diana has decided that she doesn't need a man to feel like a whole person, that she can get along and raise her children independently.

Diana Ross is still very insecure in many ways. She still wishes she had more education and sometimes feels uncomfortable around people who are better educated. She isn't very happy about getting older and worries that she's losing her looks, not realizing that the people who really matter don't care if she gets wrinkles and gray hairs. The one thing she is not insecure about is how hard she's tried and how hard she's worked to get to where she is. She knows she has done the absolute best she can, that she's never been a quitter or one to take the safe way. And so, when asked what she is most proud of, Diana Ross can think about her children and her singing and her movies and all the things that have happened to her and that she has made happen to the skinny girl from the Brewster-Douglass Projects in Detroit and she can say, thoughtfully and quietly, "I'm proud of myself."

DISCOGRAPHY

Singles and Albums That Made the
Billboard and *Cashbox* Top 100 Lists

SINGLES

Supremes (with Diana Ross)

Your Heart Belongs to Me
Let Me Go the Right Way
A Breath Taking Guy
When the Lovelight Starts Shining Through His Eyes
Run, Run, Run
Where Did Our Love Go
Baby Love
Come See About Me
Stop! In the Name of Love
Back in My Arms Again
Nothing but Heartaches
I Hear a Symphony
My World Is Empty Without You
Love Is Like an Itching in My Heart
You Can't Hurry Love
You Keep Me Hangin' On
Love Is Here and Now You're Gone
The Happening
Reflections
In and Out of Love
Forever Came Today
Some Things You Never Get Used To
Love Child
I'm Livin' in Shame
The Composer
No Matter What Sign You Are

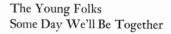

The Young Folks
Some Day We'll Be Together

Supremes (with Diana Ross) and the Temptations

I'm Gonna Make You Love Me
I'll Try Something New
The Weight

Diana Ross

Reach Out and Touch (Somebody's Hand)
Ain't No Mountain High Enough
Remember Me
Reach Out I'll Be There
Surrender
I'm Still Waiting
Good Morning Heartache
Touch Me in the Morning
Last Time I Saw Him
Sleepin'
Theme from *Mahogany* (Do You Know Where You're Going To)
Love Hangover
Gettin' Ready for Love
The Boss
I'm Coming Out
Upside Down

Diana Ross and Marvin Gaye

You're a Special Part of Me
My Mistake Was to Love You
Don't Knock My Love

ALBUMS

Supremes (with Diana Ross)

Where Did Our Love Go
A Bit of Liverpool

153

Country Western & Pop
We Remember Sam Cooke
More Hits by The Supremes
The Supremes at the Copa
I Hear a Symphony
Supremes a Go-Go
The Supremes Sing Holland-Dozier-Holland
The Supremes Sing Rodgers & Hart
Diana Ross and the Supremes Greatest Hits
Reflections
Live at London's Talk of the Town
Love Child
Let the Sunshine In
Cream of the Crop
Diana Ross & the Supremes Greatest Hits, Vol. 3

Supremes (with Diana Ross) and the Temptations

Diana Ross & the Supremes Join the Temptations
TCB
Together
On Broadway

Diana Ross

Diana Ross
Everything Is Everything
Diana (TV Soundtrack)
Surrender
Lady Sings the Blues (Original Motion Picture Soundtrack)
Touch Me in the Morning
Last Time I Saw Him
Diana Ross Live at Caesar's Palace
Diana Ross
Diana Ross' Greatest Hits
Baby It's Me
The Boss
Diana